The New Twenty

Tony Sekulich

Copyright © 2018 Tony Sekulich
All rights reserved.

ISBN-13: 9781973408642

DEDICATION

This book is dedicated to my parents, John and Dodie Sekulich. Without their continued love and support, this book would not have been possible.

CONTENTS

	Acknowledgments	I
1	Esse Quam Videri	1
2	It Isn't Ironic	39
3	The Luke & Leia Moment	79
4	Shenanigans	109
5	Up In Honey Harbour	147
6	The Six-Month Backslide	193
7	Author's Notes	241

ACKNOWLEDGMENTS

For what is generally considered to be a solo effort, the creation of this novel would not have been possible without the support, contribution, and guidance of some very key people.

There would be no such thing as The New Twenty if Dom DeLuca had not struck up a conversation with me in the summer of 2006 about working together on a project to submit to the CFC Pilot Program. We developed a script and bible that created The New Twenty universe for what exists today.

Four years later, I was looking for a producer with whom I could apply to the National Screen Institute (NSI) Totally Television Program. I briefly met Jordan Gross the year before and I approached him hoping he would partner up with me. I was confident Jordan would be a capable producer for the project. In the end, he was far more than that. He remains a friend and creative collaborator. When I am lost in the deep woods, Jordan knows how to get me back on the path. These characters and their stories would not be what they are without his guiding hand.

Speaking of the NSI, I would like to say a huge thank you to Brandice, Sam, Lauren, and everyone at the NSI who saw something in this very rough project and gave us a chance to refine it.

I also want to sincerely thank Al Magee who believed in an extremely green screenwriter and opened the doors to the Canadian Film Centre for him. Over the years, I have learned so much from him and whatever story craftsmanship is present in this book is due, in large part, to his tremendous influence. More than that, he is an amazing friend and I will treasure that friendship always.

I want to thank everyone at Wattpad for providing an outlet to share these stories with an audience. The response from readers all around the globe and how they really embraced these characters and their journeys has made this one of the most fulfilling experiences of my life. That Wattpad recognized this novel with a Watty Award is really just the icing on the cake.

I feel like I owe a debt of gratitude to someone whom I've never met but has inspired me greatly. I didn't believe there was room in the literary world for straight-out comedy novels until I started to read the works of Terry Fallis. Only after reading his comedic novels did I have the belief that there was a literary appetite for laugh-out-loud long-form writing. So thank you, Terry, for inspiring me and illuminating the path in a genre that has sorely needed a champion.

I want to express my gratitude to every single person who read and supported this book. I always wanted to see it completed as a novel but I'm not sure that ever would have happened had it not been for the very loyal and rabid fans who showed their love for it on Wattpad. That support was the fuel I needed to get it where it is today.

Lastly, I would like to thank those people who helped in preparing the book for publication. Huge thanks to Catherine Lavender, Himani Ediriweera, Twyla Andersen, Dawn Morrison, Sean Pratt, Neil Slattery, and Gillian Lisson.

To everyone who had a hand in helping this book see the light of day, I will forever be in your debt and I hope you enjoy reading the book as much as I enjoyed writing it.

Part One

ESSE QUAM VIDERI

Tony Sekulich

CHAPTER ONE

"Son of a... Why can't I see anything?"

The question is to no one in particular, yet it has deeper implications than Jeff Dempsey intends in the moment. At that precise point in time, Jeff is wondering why he's staring at a black screen and not his own image. Jeff and technology have always had a somewhat frosty relationship, so this is not new territory for him. History has taught him that there is no question too stupid to ask, no detail too simple to double check. And so, it is this train of thought that has led him to the solution.

"Did I turn the webcam on?" he asks aloud. With one keyboard click, the screen lights up and the frame is filled with the now proud and smiling face of Jeff Dempsey. If he gave it any thought at all, he would probably realize that he has little reason to feel pride, but this doesn't dampen his sense of accomplishment.

The image in the frame is that of an average looking 40-year-old man with short, sensible, dark brown hair. The only sign his youthful prime is in the rear-view mirror is the slight graying around the temples. Jeff settles in his chair, adjusts his hair, and takes a deep cleansing breath. After a few moments of quiet contemplation, Jeff begins to speak to the camera.

My favorite part of The Wizard of Oz is at the very end when Glinda the good witch tells Dorothy that she always had the power to go home. All she had to do was click her heels together. Dorothy seems to take this exceedingly well for someone who just found out that she went through six hours of unnecessary hell. But more than that, I'm fascinated by the notion that something she glanced at maybe two hundred times was exactly the key she needed, and she couldn't see it. It was right in front of her and, at the same time, invisible. In life, I'll bet that happens more than we realize.

Earlier that day...

"What did you win?" she asks with what seems to be genuine interest. Jeff heard the woman's voice, but it was not enough to snap him out of his trance-like state. Ever since he was a kid, he would slip into his own head where he would lose all contact with his immediate surroundings. Often, he would come out of it realizing he had drawn attention to himself laughing out loud at something only he could see. Other times, it's where he went when he needed sanctuary from the harsh reality of his current circumstance.

This is one of those times.

"Hello...Earth to Jeff???"

With a jolt, Jeff looks up to see Karlie, one of the wait staff at the Cedar Room Pub. The Cedar Room is another modern Irish neighborhood pub where it's not so authentic that you can only find room-temperature dark, European beers, but yet still Irish enough to make it a go-to spot every St. Patrick's Day.

Jeff and his friends discovered the Cedar Room when they were in University back in the waning days of the 20th Century. Back then, the appeal of the Cedar Room was some new promotion called *Ten-Cent Wing Night*. Given the king's ransom one now pays for a pound of chicken wings at any neighborhood pub, it's almost unfathomable that there was a time when you could fill up on wings for a couple of bucks.

Those days, like Jeff's state of mind, seem like a million miles away.

"Sorry, I was....somewhere else," he offers, hoping that she won't ask any follow-up questions.

"So, what did you win?" She gestures to the opposite side of Jeff's table.

Reluctantly, Jeff looks over and, once again, finds his gaze drawn to that which has kept him transfixed. It didn't have eyes, but still, Jeff could feel it staring through him, judging him...mocking him. The object of his obsession is a giant trophy, an obscenely large monstrosity, the kind that takes two hands to lift.

"Oh, that? That's for a...flamenco dance competition." Jeff peaks out of the corner of his eye for the tiniest sign that she is buying it. She is not. "You don't believe me?" Jeff presses.

"It's more believable than if you told me you won it at a lying competition. Another round, Señor?"

"Sí."

In a turn of fortuitous timing, Karlie heads back towards the bar just as Niko Stassinopoulos arrives. Just weeks past his 40th birthday, Niko still stands as the living embodiment of the Greek Adonis. With flawless olive skin, dark hair, and a rugged handsomeness, it would be very easy for Jeff, or any other guy for that matter, to hate him. Had they not become best friends in elementary school, well before girls entered the picture, he just might have.

Niko spots Jeff and quickly pulls up a chair at their regular table. "There you are. You flew out of there like someone put up the bat signal."

Jeff raises his near-empty beer stein. "Wherever there is an undrunk pint of beer, I will be there."

Karlie comes by with a full beer glass and 'accidentally' spills it on Niko's crotch. With a delivery usually only found in horny pizza delivery guys and naughty cheerleaders, she does a terrible job of masking her true intentions. "I'm so sorry. I don't know how that could have happened." She turns to Jeff and gives him a little wink. "I'll bring you another one, sweetie."

Jeff watches her leave to make sure she is well out of earshot before quickly spinning back to Niko. "Do you think it's possible just one time you could call a woman after you sleep with her?"

"I suppose anything's theoretically possible," Niko offers with a shrug.

"Why do you have to mess things up here? Why can't you pick up chicks at work like everybody else?"

"I teach Grade Four, you sick bastard!"

"With the other teachers or support staff!"

Karlie returns with Jeff's beer and sets it down in front of him. As she passes behind Niko, she slaps him hard on the back of the head.

"That's why," Niko says definitively.

***

On the other side of the plant-covered room divider, Ashley Holder is in the middle of a very serious conversation with her boyfriend, Greg. At 37, Ashley has a confidence about her which is evident in the way she carries herself and in the way Greg hangs on to her every word.

"So, I guess what I'm saying Greg, is that we've reached *that* point in our relationship. Do you know what I'm saying?"

"I do, Ashley. You're saying it's time that we take it to the next level." Greg gestures upwards with his hand when he says, 'next level.'

Ashley sighs and decides to try again. "Greg, I think you're a really great guy and somebody is going to be really lucky to have you."

Greg takes hold of her hands. "I think somebody already is really lucky to have me."

"Not as much as you'd think."

***

The Cedar Room doors fly open and a short, schlubby, balding man enters and rushes over to Jeff and Niko's table. This is Louie DeLulio who, like Ashley, carries himself with a great deal of confidence. But unlike Ashley, nothing he's ever accomplished in his life supports this level of confidence. Yet, he presses on, undeterred by constant failure. Louie is either the saddest or most admirable person you will ever encounter.

"Boys, I think it's really going to happen. What's the one sentence you thought you'd never hear me say?" Louie asks proudly.

"Mom, I'm moving out of your basement," Niko offers.

"No really, this one's on me," Jeff adds.

Louie should have expected that, but the jabs deflect off him like he's made of Teflon and Kevlar. Strangely, the most obvious target for derision cannot be offended. "Tomorrow, I'm going to be able to say I slept with Vicky Humphries."

Niko shakes his head. "Vicky Va-Voom? It's never going to happen."

***

Stepping up her effort to get through to Greg, Ashley is holding his hands, staring deep into his eyes, almost pleading with him. "Whenever two people start a relationship, there's only one of two ways it can end. Either they get married or they break up."

"You haven't considered death."

"I wouldn't be so sure. But what I'm saying is, I feel like we reached one of those options. You see I thi-"

Greg puts up his hands to cut her off mid-sentence. "You can stop there. I get it."

For the first time, Ashley's eyes light up with hope. "You do?"

"I do."

And just as Ashley feels like she is finally out of this conversation, she sees something that crushes those foolish hopes. Greg is suddenly beaming with joy. "I gotta go call my mom. She's going to be so excited." Greg jumps up and rushes off.

***

Louie stares at Niko, hurt and in disbelief. "It is going to happen with Vicky. She was all over me tonight. Do you know what she said as soon as she laid eyes on me?"

Louie begins recounting his experience from when he first walked in the school gym. As alumni of Holy Trinity Catholic Secondary School, the guys are invited to the reunion which is held annually in the school gymnasium. The place is decorated like a prom for 40-year-olds. There are the usual streamers and balloons in the school's navy blue and gold colors. The walls are decorated with photos and mementos from the years the alumni attended the school. With the room filled with photos of plaid shirts, ripped tights, oversized knit sweaters and Alanis Morissette playing on the sound system, it was like the 90's threw up all over the Holy Trinity gym.

The guys couldn't make their 20th reunion two years earlier and didn't bother to attend their 21st. But with Jeff going through what conservatively could be called a rough patch, Niko and Louie thought that a night out with old friends would make Jeff feel better. It was the first of many miscalculations they would make before the sun rose in the morning. At that moment, Louie thought things couldn't be going better. The first person he saw was Vicky Humphries who, at 41, still retained her blonde bombshell status. Louie describes her as if she stepped into the gym straight out of a 1980's Whitesnake video. One can almost picture her moving in slow motion, with her still strawberry blonde hair dancing as if it were being blown by a wind machine. Vicki waves as soon as she and Louie make eye contact. "It's you. I was hoping I'd see you here tonight," she says.

Louie looks to his left and right and then points to himself as if to ask 'Me?' Vicky nods and winks.

***

Louie recounts the story with conviction, but Niko's not biting. This is not the first time he's heard what sounds like a tall tale from

Louie and it would be far from the last. He gives Louie a dismissive wave. "I'm telling you, I don't see it happening."

"I'm not a high school kid anymore. Now I have the confidence to make it happen." Louie points to the Latin motto on the school crest on his name tag. "*Esse Quam Videri.* Seize the day."

Niko scoffs at this. "Are you drunk? That doesn't mean seize the day."

"Well, what do you think it means?" Louie counters.

"We went to Catholic school, so I think it means panties optional."

"Well, it means seize the day to me."

Jeff tried his best to stay out of this, but now he's heard enough. "No. If you're going to make me sit here and listen to this inane rambling, we're going to get it right. Carpe Diem means seize the day."

"Then what does Esse Quam Videri mean?" Louie asks.

Silence hangs in the air before a female voice from the other side of the divider pipes up, "To be rather than to seem."

The guys look over to find Ashley standing up and giving them a little wave. "Sorry, I couldn't help but overhear."

Jeff looks at her for a second and while she looks familiar, he can't seem to place her. "Do I know you?"

"I'm Ashley."

"I'm Jeff. This is Niko and Louie."

Louie steers the conversation back to what he believes is the most pressing matter at the moment. "Why do you think I can't hook up with Vicky Humphries?"

"Because I have dibs," Niko offers matter-of-factly.

"It's true. He called dibs on her back in high school," Jeff says.

Louie makes a face. "That doesn't count now." Louie turns to Ashley for support. "Tell him."

Now Ashley makes a disapproving face. "Wait, what is dibs? Please tell me it's not what it sounds like."

"Niko called dibs on her so that means we have to back off from actively pursuing her," Jeff explains.

"So, one of you calls dibs and now he owns this woman?"

"Of course not," Jeff quickly replies.

"He owns her rights," Louie clarifies.

"It's a thing that guys do to stop us from destroying each other over a woman, that's all," Jeff offers.

***

Greg comes bounding back into the bar. He is almost gliding on air with joy. "Ashley, sweetie. My mom is super excited, we're thinking about maybe a fall wedding."

Ashley leans into the guys. "Looks like I've got to take care of a dibs situation of my own. Nice to see you again, Jeff." She disappears back behind the divider.

Niko approaches Jeff and puts his hand on Jeff's shoulder. The gesture is a small one but it also represents the furthest two guys can go in terms of physical intimacy before things get officially weird. Niko is doing everything he can to pull Jeff out of the tailspin he currently finds himself in. "Come on, buddy. Let's go back to the reunion."

Jeff just shakes his head. "I can't go back there."

"Not even to be my wingman?" Louie asks.

"Sorry, Lou."

Niko has known Jeff long enough to know there is no way Jeff is going to be convinced. Niko still remembers the now infamous 'A-Team incident' of 1983 when a seven-year-old Jeff refused to watch their favourite show after the TV was moved from the living room to the family den. It didn't matter that the den was newly decorated with the coolest leather furniture and a color TV so big, its picture so clear, you could practically taste George Peppard's cigar. That was all secondary to the point that Jeff watches the A-Team in the living room. It would be six weeks before Jeff would relent. Having lived through that, Niko knew it was time to cut bait and move on.

"Come on Louie, let's go back. I have to stop off at my place first and change my pants."

Louie looks down at Niko's pants and does a double take. "Did you just piss yourself?"

"If only," Niko sighs as they walk out the door.

***

Ashley has abandoned all hope Greg will read between the lines. She should have known better. He's always been a kind and considerate boyfriend but there are times he comes across denser than an Amazonian rain forest. His inability to read the room is one of the reasons she finds herself having this conversation in the first place.

"Greg. You have to listen to me. There's not going to be a fall wedding."

With the silent mocking presence of the trophy being his only distraction, Jeff has no choice but to overhear the conversation taking place next to him. Anyone casting even a casual glance his way could tell how he feels about it. Jeff's poker face is rivaled only by Greg's ability to take a hint.

"So, we have a long engagement, that's fine with me as long as we are together."

Jeff's face contorts ever so slightly.

"That's not what I'm saying. I don't see it working out between us. There's not a future there," Ashley blurts out.

"I don't understand," Greg responds with just a hint of whining in his voice.

Almost involuntarily, Jeff pushes his chair from the table and stands up with such force that the chair goes tumbling behind him. He marches over to Ashley's table and pulls up a chair and sits on it backwards so he's leaning up against the back of the chair.

"I can't listen to this one second longer. Let me see if I can help," he says to Ashley, sounding both pained and apologetic. He then turns his full attention to Greg. "Knock. Knock."

Greg knows how to respond but he's not sure if he wants to. He looks pleadingly at Ashley who averts her gaze, offering him no help whatsoever. Reluctantly, he looks back to Jeff. "Who's there?"

"Not you anymore. You're dumped. Whatever you think you still have, you don't. It's over. Now build a bridge - get over it!"

Neither Greg nor Ashley quite know how to respond to this. With his work here done, Jeff proudly stands up and heads back to his seat but not before giving Ashley a little 'you're welcome' wink. As Jeff settles in and signals to Karlie for another round, a devastated Greg rushes out the front door. Now it's Ashley who is making a beeline over to Jeff. Jeff sees her approach and politely waves her off.

"No need to thank me," he offers in his best awe-shucks-just-doing-my-job-ma'am tone.

"Thank you?!?" Ashley spits out as both question and statement of righteous indignation.

"You're welcome," Jeff offers, totally unaware of the irony in completely misreading the intent behind Ashley's words.

"I didn't need your help. I think I know how to break up with a guy."

"No, you did a great job. The wedding planner he hired thought so too."

"Maybe next time you can just let me handle it."

"I'm sorry but after the last couple of weeks I've had, I couldn't listen to that break-up any longer."

"What happened? Did you have a 'dibs' situation go bad?"

"You could say that." Jeff hadn't planned on talking about it, so he thinks carefully about whether he wants to continue. He takes a huge swig of the fresh beer Karlie dropped on the table to buy time. He didn't come to the Cedar Room in search of a therapy session but, for some reason, he finds himself willing to open up to Ashley. At least more than he did with the guys. "I came home to find my wife of 20 years with her suitcases packed and waiting for me at the front door. Like your friend there, I never saw it coming."

Jeff begins to tell Ashley about the time he and Ellen spent together. He describes a class where each person is working on a piece of art. Jeff is working on a painting while Ellen works away on her own right beside him.

"I met Ellen in the first week of my first year of university and we got married the weekend we graduated. From the day we met, we did everything together."

Ellen shows her painting to Jeff who smiles broadly when he sees it. He nods in pleasant approval.

Jeff then tells Ashley about their regular game night. He describes he and Ellen seated at their dining room table, engaged in a game of Scrabble.

"We liked to wind down the weekend with Scrabble Sundays. Ellen's pretty tough to beat. I don't know where she comes up with some of those words."

Ellen plays a word and Jeff smiles and nods in approval. He gestures tipping his cap to her.

Ashley sits down across from Jeff. "I'm so sorry. Is that why you can't go to your reunion?"

"Actually, that's not why I can't go back."

"Then what is it?"

Once again, Louie comes barreling through the front door. "Jeff, I need a dibs ruling."

Jeff holds out his hand in Louie's direction. "Well, for one thing..."

As per usual, Louie carries on, oblivious to whatever situation he may be rampaging through. "I need you to rule statue of limitations."

As soon as it hits her ear, Ashley cocks her head like a curious Scottish Terrier. "Did he just say *statue* of limitations?"

"He did but that's not the bone I have to pick right now. Surely, with all the crap I'm dealing with, you guys are not going to put me in the middle of your dibs squabble."

Before Louie can answer, Niko bursts through the front door with the same willful disregard for whatever may be happening at the moment. "Don't listen to him. Just tell him there is no <u>statute</u> of limitations in dibs."

Jeff sighs in resignation. "He's right. Niko has dibs indefinitely until Vicky either tells him he doesn't have a shot with her or Niko relinquishes dibs voluntarily."

"You guys have a whole set of rules to this thing?" Ashley asks, still barely able to wrap her mind around this testosterone-driven ritual.

"Dibs is a long-standing sacred pact between guys," Niko says.

Jeff is desperate to extricate himself from this nonsense. "Are we good now because, as God is my witness, I cannot think of a conversation I'd least like to be a part of right now."

As Jeff talks, Niko and Louie look towards the doorway and simultaneously show expressions of deep concern. Niko cautiously nudges Jeff and gestures towards the bar's front door. "I can think of one."

Jeff turns around and sees his soon-to-be-ex Ellen standing in the doorway.

CHAPTER TWO

It's amazing how many thoughts can go through your mind in a matter of milliseconds. From the time Jeff first spotted Ellen to the time his legs kicked into overdrive and propelled him around the nearest corner, no more than 1.3 seconds elapsed. And yet, in that time, Jeff entertained the following questions: What is she doing here? Is she looking for me? Why is she looking for me? What if she's not here for me and is on a date? Why is God punishing me? Is there a nearby speeding train I can hurl myself either in front of or under?

Before Jeff can ponder the answer to any of the above questions, he finds himself standing in front of the washrooms, safely out of sight, but seriously out of breath. Ashley, Niko and Louie soon join him. Ashley eyes him up down. "You aren't hiding from her, are you?"

"Absolutely not. I'm simply pondering the best course of action."

"You're going to sneak out."

"Out the nearest open window."

For all their ridiculously self-absorbed tendencies, Louie and Niko are still able to step up for a buddy in a crisis situation. One look into Jeff's wide, panicked eyes was all they needed to spring into action. One advantage of being bar regulars is knowing the floor plan by heart. This is not the first time a surprise visitor triggered an emergency evacuation. In fact, for Niko, this happens at a greater frequency than Margarita Mondays. They both quickly bolt for the door to the back entrance. Within seconds, Niko returns shaking his head.

"There are no open windows, and the back door is chained. We're going to have to get you out the front door," Niko concludes.

"We're going to need a diversion," Jeff says.

Whether they were genuinely considering other options, or just going through the motions, it wasn't long before the guys all came to the same conclusion. They all stand there with their gazes fixed on Ashley. She immediately shakes her head repeatedly in protest.

"No. No. No. I don't even know her. What would I do?"

A few seconds of silence elapse before Niko offers a solution. "Hit on her."

Louie is immediately on board. "Ooooh, yeah!" As his words hang in the air, it is clear the response blew well past 'enthusiastic support and crossed into 'unhealthy perversion.'

Not surprisingly, the plan did not have unanimous buy-in. "I'm not going to hit on her!"

It is only moments before Ellen will discover their presence and they don't have the luxury of time to continue this debate. One can only guess that's what Niko tells himself to justify what he's about to do next. "Well, you better think of something," he says as he shoves Ashley out into the main bar area and blocks her path to return to the safety of the washroom corridor. Ashley shoots Niko the female death glare that often reduces men to groveling masses of jelly. Clearly, Ashley intends to pick this up at a later date. For now, without another plan to follow, she reluctantly approaches Ellen who is standing at the front bar.

She sidles up to Ellen, looks directly at her, but says nothing. Ellen finally notices the strange woman staring at her.

"Hello?" Ellen says in a can-I-help-you manner.

In the background, Niko and Louie emerge with Jeff who has a jacket draped over his head. Clearly, this represents their best attempt at remaining inconspicuous. From her angle, Ashley can see the guys but Ellen cannot. Ashley does her best to sound casual. "Hi."

There was a moment of an awkward silence. "Can I help you with something?" Ellen asks. She starts to glance around the room so Ashley acts quickly to recapture her attention. She starts rubbing Ellen's blouse.

"I love this material. It's so soft."

"Thank you," Ellen says cautiously.

"It looks great on you. It really complements your figure. God, you have such a great body."

Upon hearing that last statement, they guys stop their trek towards the front door and stand there caught up in Ashley's attempt at seduction.

"Um...thanks," Ellen says, unable to disguise her growing discomfort.

Ashley discreetly but frantically waves for the guys to get outside. They shuffle out the front door.

***

To the casual observer, the feat they just pulled off would hardly register as noteworthy. After all, they merely orchestrated a very crude distraction and waltzed out the front door. It's not exactly Steve McQueen jumping the Nazi prison fence on his motorcycle. Still, standing beneath the towering oak trees in the downtown city square, Jeff is awash in the most joy and relief he's felt in weeks.

"Better than the bus pull," Louie chimes in as he high-fives Jeff.

Louie's comment triggers a series of memories of other great moments Jeff's experienced in the downtown square. If he had to rank them, this was the second best feeling he's had there. Topping the list is the aforementioned bus pull where teams from rival high schools competed to see who could pull a city transit bus up the steepest downtown street the fastest. Jeff was a member of the winning team in his Grade-Ten year and the sheer euphoria he experienced was surprising even to him, given how silly the event was. He had no idea it was a simple product of biochemistry, an exercise-induced release of endorphins in the brain. All he knew was, at that moment, jumping into the arms of his classmates, it was the closest he ever came to feel what it would be like to win the Stanley Cup.

Jeff was smiling, lost in that memory when Niko brought him crashing back to Earth. "So, we can't talk you into going back to the reunion?"

Jeff just turns and looks away, unable to make eye contact. Out of the corner of his eye, he sees Ashley approaching with Jeff's trophy in hand. "Go on without me. I'll be okay."

Niko and Louie exchange looks and come to the same silent conclusion – no sense in pressing him. They're not going to get anywhere.

As they walk off, Louie feels compelled to draw the battle lines. "Just so you know, I'm going after Vicky."

"You're not respecting dibs?"

"Nope!"

"You realize this means war."

"Bring it on."

Ashley arrives with the look one would have if they just did five to 10 years in a federal penitentiary after taking the fall for the other members of the team – bitter, jaded with a well-earned sense of entitlement. She drops the trophy at his feet.

"So, I'm pretty sure I just earned my first restraining order. You want to tell me what this is all about?"

"Not particularly."

"Let's try this again, only not phrased as a question. Start talking immediately about what has you so spooked about seeing your old classmates? I mean, they gave you this huge trophy."

"The trophy is the reason."

Jeff begins telling Ashley where the story all began. He sets the scene by describing how he, Niko, and Louie were sitting in Niko's living room which looked more like a university dorm room. Full and empty bottles of beer and pizza boxes were strewn around the place. It's obvious they'd been enjoying themselves for a while.

"It was a week or so after Ellen left and the boys were helping me get through it the only way we knew how – drink through it. It happened to be the same day the reunion information forms came in the mail. Every year they have these stupid awards like 'travelled farthest' or 'has the most kids'. Nobody takes them seriously and I wasn't happy with my current lot in life so Niko had an idea.

"Make stuff up," Niko offers.

"I can't do that!"

"Sure you can. Watch this." Niko grabs a piece of paper off the coffee table and starts to write down what he says out loud.

"Occupation. Jeff considers..."

Jeff's recounting of the incident picks up at the reunion where Tracey, 41, a prim and proper looking woman, reads out Jeff's information at the reunion. She picks up where Niko left off.

"...his life's vocation to be helping the underprivileged. To this end, he gave up his lucrative medical practice to work with malnourished and medically deprived children in the third world." She takes a short but noticeable pause before continuing. "Plus, he gives free boob jobs to unattractive foreign chicks who are too flat-chested to find a husband in their village."

Ashley's reaction punctures Jeff's story. "Wait, what!?!"

Back to the night in Niko's apartment, Jeff and Niko's heads snap around and they stare at Louie.

"Wait, what!?!" Niko and Jeff blurt out in unison.

Louie stands his ground, vociferously defending the added section. "It's good. It makes him look sensitive to women's issues. I'm putting it in." Louie grabs the form and the pen and enthusiastically writes it down.

"After that, we just went with it," Jeff offers by way of explanation.

Jeff continues recounting the events of earlier in the evening for Ashley. She processes the remainder of Tracey's speech about Jeff as a montage of bite-sized information chunks.

"...built the first primary school in a village 100 kilometers east of Kuala Lumpur..."

"...taught sign language to the hearing impaired in the mountain regions of Peru."

"...married to a lingerie model/fantasy football expert who likes to spend her spare time perfecting the ultimate BBQ ribs."

Once again, Ashley somehow has him sharing more than he originally intended. But now it has taken on a momentum of its own and Jeff is no longer fighting it.

"It was a drunken lapse in judgment. I didn't know they were going to make a big deal out of it...and it gets worse."

"It can't"

"Tracey is my ex-girlfriend. We dated all through Grade 12. I went through that whole humiliating charade in front of the one person I wanted to impress."

"I stand corrected. You've managed to prove two things. There is a God and he hates you."

***

Niko is engaged in a deep conversation with Vicky about kids today and how truly terrible their music is when he spots something that gives him pause. It's Louie standing by himself, grinning like an idiot. It's a look Niko has seen too many times before. This is Louie's I-have-a-brilliant-plan-up-my-sleeve look. The last time Louie had this look, he and Niko spent an entire night being interrogated by border guards as to why they had a trunk full of Chinese bootleg DVD's. They weren't charged formally but can now boast about being on an international contraband watch list. On this night, Niko didn't know what was coming; he just knew it wasn't going to be good.

Louie approaches them and smiles politely, too politely for Niko's liking. "Lovely evening tonight, it sure is great to see everyone again," Louie says.

"Yes, it is," Niko cautiously replies.

Louie looks over Vicky's shoulder and squints as if he's trying to lock in on something. "Is that Jimmy Tate? I thought he had moved to the States."

When Vicky turns away to take a closer look, Louie grabs a nearby glass of ice water off a table and throws it on Niko's pants making it look like he wet himself. When Vicky turns back, Louie puts on his best empathetic face. He leans into Niko and half-whispers, making sure he's still loud enough for Vicky to hear. "Dude, I think you had another one of your accidents."

Vicky looks down and is clearly grossed out. Niko glares at Louie then goes off to dry himself. Louie takes Vicky by the arm as if he were at an 1878 Savannah cotillion and escorts her away. "Let me apologize for my friend's...bladder control problem. He's quite sensitive about it."

***

Outside in the city square, Ashley can no longer contain her curiosity about the relevance of the trophy in the night's predicament. She picks it and examines it closely. "Are we almost at the point where the trophy comes into the picture?"

"Remember how I said they give out these stupid awards? Well, there's one that isn't quite so stupid," Jeff says. As Jeff recounts the story, Ashley is transported back to earlier that night where Tracey stands at the podium on the stage.

"Here at Holy Trinity, we're proud of all our alumni but there are those special few who have gone on to inspire others. We have two wonderful nominees for 'Most Inspirational'. We've already heard about the tremendous work Jeff Dempsey has been doing around the globe. Our second nominee is joining us on a brief reprieve from the Intensive Care Unit. Please take a look at the inspirational story of Dennis Bruce.

As soon as the words 'intensive care unit' hit Jeff's ears, a sense of terror overtakes him. "Oh, no," he says involuntarily.

Just hearing the story, Ashley has a similar reaction. "Oh, no!"

"Oh, yes," Jeff affirms as he continues on.

As Tracey finishes teeing up Dennis Bruce's candidacy, a video appears on a giant video screen behind the stage. It shows a very frail and sickly Dennis, getting treatment in the hospital for something called Roderick's Syndrome. Roderick's Syndrome is explained as a rare but devastating neuro-muscular affliction. This is followed by a clip that shows Dennis reading to sick kids. Another clip explains that his whole life doesn't revolve around his illness. It shows Dennis running a midnight basketball league for inner-city youth. A final clip shows Dennis volunteering at the soup kitchen. When the clips are done, his classmates acknowledge Dennis who pushes himself away from the table, revealing he is currently in a wheelchair.

"I wish we had two awards to give out but since we have only one, this year's Most Inspirational goes to...Jeff Dempsey," Tracey proudly announces.

"Let me get this straight," Ashley says walking right up to Jeff. "You cheated a chronically ill, wheelchair-bound, soup kitchen volunteer out of a humanitarian award!?!"

"I know, it's one of those moral gray areas," Jeff shrugs.

"Moral gray area?!? I can't imagine a crasser, more self-serving stunt someone could pull at a high-school reunion."

***

While Louie's plan may have involved the subtlety and deft touch of a wrecking ball, it did enjoy a certain measure of success.

Louie is chatting privately with Vicky in a quiet corner of the gym. This is going well, Louie thought to himself. Almost too well. Louie has a terrible feeling there is going to be a retaliatory strike coming but he doesn't know when or from where. He wouldn't have to wait long to find out.

Tracey steps up to the microphone on the stage and taps it to make sure it is on. "Hi everyone, it looks like we're in for a surprise treat. One of our very own wants to play a song he wrote. Let's all welcome Niko Stassinopoulos."

Louie stops whatever point he was making and instantly turns his full attention to what is taking place on stage.

"I didn't know Niko was a musician," Vicky says.

"I didn't either," Louie says trying to mask the terror that has overtaken him.

On stage, Niko tunes his guitar, slowly and methodically. To the outside observer, this is the simple act of a master musician making sure his instrument is in top form before he performs. Louie knows better. This is the work of a master sadist making sure he extracts every last ounce of agony from his victim. And it's working.

"This is a song that goes out to a friend of mine," Niko says casually. "And he knows why."

Louie is suddenly very concerned. Niko begins playing the opening chords of what sounds like a 1960's folk song. It's what Woody Guthrie would have written if he were petty, vindictive, and hell-bent to screw over a buddy.

"He's a complicated man, there's not a lot who know him. He'd rather keep his cards real close, doesn't like to show 'em."

Louie's okay with this so far. This might not be as bad as he first feared.

"If anyone found out, they'll say I'm gone, I'll see ya. Cause my friend Louie has Gonorrhea."

"And there it is," Louie says aloud. He peeks out the corner of his eye to see how Vicky is reacting. Not surprisingly, Vicky has a disturbed look on her face. Niko ramps up to the repetitive chorus.

"Yeah, my friend Louie has Gonorrhea. Sayin' my friend Louie has Gonorrhea. Oh, my friend Louie has Gonorrhea. Tellin' you, my friend Louie has Gonorrhea."

There is now a distance between Louie and Vicky.

***

Perhaps the only person in the city more ill-at-ease than Louie at that precise moment is Jeff who paces around the city square, clearly wound up. Now that Ashley managed to get Jeff talking about what happened, he's showing no signs of stopping anytime soon.

"I know it was a stupid thing to do but I just couldn't go back there and face those people as I am – a textbook example of unfulfilled potential."

"Is that really how you see yourself?"

The question catches Jeff like a boxer struck by a quick left jab to the jaw. It rocks him and leaves him discombobulated for a few seconds. He has to think for a few moments before he can respond with a coherent answer. He paces back and forth for about 10 seconds before he settles in front of Ashley and raises his gaze to meet hers.

"I used to be something in high school. I led our basketball team to the championship. I once scored 51 points against St. John's and...

"It was against Franklin Heights," Ashley interjects.

Jeff is more than a little annoyed. Not because she interrupted his train of thought, but because she did so while being completely wrong. The 51-point game was the highlight of a high school career that was chock full of them. It was one of those only-happens-in the-movies moments that happened in real life. Why would a complete stranger feel like she knew what happened better than he? Accordingly, Jeff is unable to quell his patronizing tone. "Um...hello! I was there. It was against St. John's."

Ashley rolls her eyes but doesn't press it any further. Jeff is really feeling it now and the last thing she wants to do is derail him.

"The point is, I'm not even close to being the man I wanted to be."

"Tell me about him."

Bam! There's another left jab. How is she doing this?

"The man you wanted to be," Ashley continues. "Picture him as a completely separate entity from yourself and describe him."

For a moment, Jeff considers pulling the pin on this entire line of questioning. He didn't plan on doing this much introspection when the day began. Although, if he really thought about it, there's probably not one thing that's happened so far today that's gone according to plan. The plan hasn't worked for him so far so he figures there's no harm in playing along. Once again, he starts to pace and talk.

"He's got a great career that he loves, spends time with his friends, takes time to travel, has someone truly special in his life who he cherishes, he acts, ice skates, volunteers his time." The more Jeff describes him, the more this person sounds like a completely fictional character. This brings a certain sadness that sits like a rock in his gut.

"So, what's stopping you from being that guy?"

Jeff is growing tired of these simple yet enlightening questions. His answers are becoming more curt. "I'm almost 40. It's too late." Jeff is hoping she will accept this as an answer and let it go. Deep down, of course, he knows better.

"It's not. It's simple really. All you have to do is do one thing every day that the old you would be too afraid to do. Do you think you can do that?"

"I suppose but-"

"Good. We start now. Grab your trophy."

Jeff is now completely turned around in his head. Is this some kind self-reflection exercise? His curiosity gets the best of him. "Why would I do that?"

"Because we're going back to your high school reunion."

CHAPTER THREE

Jeff walks inside the doors of Holy Trinity School and suddenly stops as Ashley continues walking ahead. It isn't clear whether Jeff is having second thoughts or if his abrupt halt was involuntary – a terror-induced temporary paralysis. There's no question there were only a handful of things Jeff would find more unpleasant than walking back into that gym. As he quickly compiled that list in his head, he immediately came up with: *A Real Housewives of...anywhere* marathon, six days trapped in an elevator with Zamfir, master of the pan flute, and three physical acts so vile and stomach-churning, he could not express them aloud out of respect for community standards of public decency. Eventually, Ashley notices Jeff has fallen behind and takes a few steps towards him, prepared to physically escort him inside if necessary. She hopes it won't come to that.

"So, we're agreed?" she asks, half-pleadingly.

"That Caddyshack II is so bad it deserves to be recognized as a global atrocity through a joint United Nations resolution? Absolutely," Jeff offers.

"That you apologize for earlier tonight and renounce the trophy," Ashley replies.

"Yeah, I was afraid that's what you were talking about."

Jeff inhales deeply and mentally prepares himself for walking back into his high school reunion. After a few moments of reflection, Jeff is able to get his legs working once again and he starts towards the gym doors. Before he can get there, he is intercepted by a sight that makes him immediately reconsider his stance on Zamfir and two of the three vile acts. Dennis Bruce wheels by and parks his wheelchair in their immediate path, giving them no option but to stop and greet him. Jeff and Dennis lock eyes; the tension between them is palpable.

"Dennis."

"Jeffery."

A few more seconds of stare-down before Dennis rolls away. "Good Lord! How can someone so close to death muster up so much hatred and contempt for me?" Jeff asks.

"Gee, I wonder what it could be," Ashley replies with as much sarcasm as she can get away with without sending Jeff running out the door.

***

Louie is standing in the corridor just outside the gym when Niko walks up to him. They greet each other with the subtlest of nods, not unlike two opposing power attorneys before heading into the courtroom. Neither is willing to lower his guard just yet.

"So, Vicky must think we're quite the pair," Niko offers as a trial balloon. It works. Louie loosened up enough to allow himself a tiny chuckle.

"Yeah, between your bladder control issues and my STD, I'm sure she's weak in the knees." The guys now share a laugh over this. "You realize we're on a path of mutually assured destruction," Louie cautions.

"I know. If we don't stop this soon, neither one of us will have a shot with her."

"Or worse, we might not be speaking to each other. But I'm not ready to give up and you have dibs so what can we do?"

Niko has an idea. "Make me an offer."

***

Standing inside the gym, Jeff finds himself struggling with the weight, both actual and karmic, of that huge, shiny albatross. Giving the trophy back and getting out of there as quickly as possible is Jeff's only goal. Fortunately, he spots the one person who might be able to facilitate this. Jeff approaches Tracey and leans in to whisper in her ear.

"I didn't get a chance to say it before but you still look great," he says gently.

"Thank you. And congratulations. You've really changed since we were a couple. I'd love to meet this lingerie model wife of yours."

"Yeah, me too," he says immediately recognizing the lunacy in that statement. He plows ahead, hoping she won't notice. "I was wondering if I might be able to say a few words to the class."

Before she can answer, Brent, a balding, bespectacled insurance salesman comes by and throws his arm around Jeff's shoulder. "Jeff buddy, come on!" Brent starts pulling him up towards the stage. "They're honoring our varsity basketball championship!"

Brent pulls Jeff up on to the stage. Within moments, they are joined by rest of the varsity basketball team. This moment marks the first time these 12 guys have been together since the 'come to Jesus' party where they celebrated the provincial championship. The party got its name from the Purple Jesus drink the boys pounded all night. A Purple Jesus is an extremely potent combination of grape juice, ginger ale, and whatever hard liquor is brought to the party. So, the boys came to Jesus all through that night. After which, Jesus rose again in the form of alcohol-induced vomiting in the early morning hours, the late morning hours, well into the afternoon hours, followed by the dry heaves clear into the following night. In actual fact, the party really should have been called the 'Please Jesus, either kill me or make this puking stop' party as this was a sentiment expressed by more than one champion basketball player the following day.

But even that awful memory makes Jeff smile, which is something he didn't think would be possible just ten minutes earlier. Brent takes the microphone at the podium and begins commenting on a video montage which is showing highlights of that championship run. Many of the clips feature a young and spry Jeff Dempsey.

"Watch this steal and no-look pass by Junior!" The crowd cheers. Jeff lets out a fist pump.

"Down by two, less than five seconds to go. Dempsey launches a three and...MONEY. That one got us in the playoffs," Brent says inciting an even bigger cheer from their classmates. Jeff is feeding off this energy, he's really into it.

"And who could ever forget Jeff Dempsey's 51-point game against Franklin Heights in the semis."

The crowd goes crazy both in the gym and on the video. But Jeff's head snaps around when Brent says Franklin Heights. He's confused and finds himself bombarded by several questions which all occur to him at once. How can this be? Wasn't the 51-point game against St. John's? And how did Ashley know when-

"I was told Jeff wanted to say a few words. Jeff, come on up," Brent says.

Brent's call for him to speak prevents Jeff from giving any further thought to the barrage of internal questions. Jeff has to put that aside for the moment and think about what he's going to say to the now raucous crowd.

"That was pretty awesome, huh!" The crowd cheers again. Jeff got a bit of jolt from that boisterous reaction.

"What I wanted to say is...ST. JOHN'S CAN SUCK IT!"

Again, they cheer wildly! Everyone except Ashley who buries her face in her hands, unable to watch. What is he doing, she thinks to herself.

"FRANKLIN HEIGHTS CAN SUCK IT!" More wild cheers. Jeff is now caught up in wave even he cannot rein in now. "DENNIS BRUCE CAN SUCK IT!"

This last statement is met by dead silence and blank stares. Then...wild cheers!

Jeff and his teammates are as happy as they've been in years as they exit the stage together. Desperate for one last glimpse of his youthful glory, Jeff turns back to the screen and that is when he finally sees it. There, in the bottom corner of the frozen frame, is the unmistakable image of a young and gangly Ashley sitting on the team bench. Jeff is suddenly hit by quick flashbacks

He's immediately brought back to saying goodbye after their initial conversation in the Cedar Room earlier that night.

"Nice to see you again, Jeff."

Then again speaking with her in the city square.

"I once scored 51 points against St. John's." "It was against Franklin Heights."

Jeff rushes off the stage and goes over to find Ashley. "We went to school together."

Ashley looks at him quizzically for a moment. "Mountains are tall."

Now Jeff looks at her blankly.

"I'm sorry I thought we were playing the state-the-obvious game," Ashley explains. "I was the equipment manager when you played varsity in senior year."

"No, that can't be. I remember that girl. I think her name was Ginny. Ginny Holder."

Ashley holds out her hand. "Virginia Ashley Holder. Nice to meet you."

Jeff now looks at her as if he's seeing her for the first time. "Wow. You're not a..."

"Geeky insecure tenth grader anymore. Thanks."

Jeff can't shake the feeling he's been sucked into an episode of *The X-Files*. Every answer only leads to more questions. And while Jeff had no shortage from which to choose, only one seemed most pressing at the time. "Why are you doing all this for me?"

"Because four and a half years ago, I was Jeff Dempsey. Or at least the broken shell of him that's standing before me."

Jeff is a bit stung but doesn't let it show. He's more than eager to hear where she's going with this.

"I celebrated my 34th birthday alone, in a restaurant, crying. When the waiter took pity on me and didn't charge me for the bottle of champagne I ordered to share with my friends who didn't show up, that was one of the highlights of my year. My husband ended our eight-year marriage because one day he realized that his hot blonde 23-year-old assistant 'just gets him.' I was stuck in a sales job that I hated but had no idea how to leave. Luckily my boss made that process easy for me when he fired me for poor performance. So yeah, I know the deep hole you're in, Jeff. And, more importantly, I know how to get out."

"How?"

"I did two things for myself every day. For one, I made sure I did one thing the old me was too afraid to do. It was hard at first but that process eventually led me to life coaching which is what I do for a living now. One day I woke up and realized that I was happy, confident and light years away from the person I was before. And that's when I started going by my middle name. Ginny was someone I didn't want to be anymore."

Jeff just stares at her, lost for words.

"You can be the new Jeff Dempsey. But you have to stop running and hiding. Really look at your life in a brutally honest way and you'll know what you have to do. We're adults Jeff, not children. It's time to start acting like it."

Before Jeff can give that any thought, Louie rushes up to him almost out of breath. "Jeff, Niko is willing to give up dibs on the hot chick but he wants me to trade some of my cool stuff."

Jeff looks at Ashley with a sheepish look and a bit of shrug. As always, Louie powers on. "He'll give me dibs but he wants veto power over the next three women I call dibs on, my Springsteen vinyl collection and a steak dinner at a restaurant to be named later."

Jeff is quick to respond. "Springsteen on vinyl is a non-starter. You'll offer him veto on the next woman you call dibs on, your Hall & Oates collection and lunch at a restaurant of your choice."

"That's great," Louie beams. "You're an awesome guy, Jeff. I don't know why Ellen called you overbearing." Louie runs off excited. Jeff feels as if that boxer gave up on the left jabs and connected with the roundhouse right cross.

And that's when it hit me. I don't know if it was Ashley's challenge to look at my life in a brutally honest way or that Ellen found me overbearing but all of a sudden, I was seeing things I never saw before.

Jeff is picturing the scene he described to Ashley earlier where he and Ellen are taking art classes. Once again Jeff pictures Ellen showing her painting to him as Jeff smiles broadly upon seeing it. Only this time, Jeff is noticing what she has painted. It's an image of Ellen looking out the window of a suburban house. The house has bars in the window and a huge barbed-wire fence surrounding it. Jeff feels like an idiot as he sees his previous self just smiling and nodding in approval. He can now recall how Ellen looked at him incredulously.

In an instant, he's back to the time he and Ellen are seated at their dining room table playing Scrabble. For the first time, Jeff is recalling the word that Ellen spells out on the board: D-E-S-P-A-I-R. Also on the board are MONOTONY and ESCAPE.

Jeff looks at Ashley like a man who's feeling the earth crumble beneath his feet. "How did I not see it coming?"

***

Niko and Louie are staring at each other in what appears to be the latter stages of tense negotiations. "Hall & Oates?" Niko says with a scoff. "You can't come to me with Hall & Oates."

"I can't budge on Springsteen."

Niko sighs. "I'm a friend so here's what I'm prepared to do. Veto power over the next two women you call dibs on, dinner at a steakhouse of my choosing and your Tom Petty and the Heartbreakers vinyl collection."

Louie considers this for a few seconds. It's asking a lot but when he thinks about the night he's about to have in return, he quickly spits out his answer. "Deal."

"Fine, I relinquish dibs."

***

Jeff picks up his trophy and notices it feels lighter for some reason. It could be the surge of adrenaline that is rushing through him at that moment or perhaps the recent revelations have lifted a weight from him in more ways than one. Regardless of the how or why, Jeff carries the trophy up on the stage and taps the microphone to make sure it's on.

Some in the crowd start chanting. "Jeff! Jeff! Jeff!" He waves them off and holds up the trophy.

"I don't deserve this and I can't accept it. I'm not a doctor, I don't help anyone and I'm not married to a lingerie model."

From his vantage point off to the side of the stage, this is the greatest thing Dennis Bruce has ever seen. His smug grin can be seen from space.

"I said all those things on my form because I didn't want to come here and face you all as who I really am. Another divorced 40-year-old who never lived up to his potential and whose best days are behind him."

Jeff now has the complete attention of his classmates who look on in stunned silence.

"There's just this expectation that we all have to show up here and talk about how our lives worked out perfectly. Perfect job, perfect home, perfect spouse. Well, life doesn't always work out that way. So, I'm trying to take an honest look at my life and take stock of all the things I could do better. It's not just me, right? I'm sure there are a lot of you out there who would like to change some aspect of your life."

A man's voice rises up from the crowd. "I have a gambling problem!"

Then a woman. "My kids are awful. I can't wait for them to move out."

Jeff is overcome by a sense of joy and relief. "Yes! Yes, that's it!"

"I like to watch old Menudo videos and touch myself," another voice loudly confesses.

"Okay, maybe that's enough with the sharing," Jeff says waving his hands as if to signal enough. "The point is, it's not too late to still become that person we all wanted to be."

Jeff looks out to find Ashley before continuing. "And with just a little bit of help from a new friend, I can still fulfill the potential you saw in the 17-year-old in those clips earlier tonight. Because who says 40 has to mean your best days are behind you? For us, 40 is the new 20!"

Immediately after Jeff finishes his speech, he closes his eyes. Partially out of complete emotional exhaustion and partly out of fear for what might happen next. What did happen next was beyond his wildest dreams. The room erupted in thunderous applause. Tracey joins him on the stage and picks up the trophy.

"I think this belongs to you," she says smiling.

And that was my ruby slippers moment. I had been exposed to the notion of Esse Quam Videri my whole life but never really got it until that very moment. How all the trophies and accolades in the world can never equal one genuine moment of honesty and courage. Of course, not everybody saw it this way.

Over at his table, Dennis has seen more than he can handle. He is overcome with incredulous rage.

"This....is.... BULLSHIT!"

Dennis pushes himself away from the table and tries to flip over the table. Of course, given his physical affliction, he lacks the strength to do it with adequate force. He struggles mightily but is unable to lift the legs even a millimeter off the floor. What is supposed to come off as blind rage is more adorable and just a little sad. He starts to wheel himself towards the exit.

"I'm the inspirational one," he shouts to anyone within earshot. He does the only damage he can do - knocking over a flower arrangement and a lectern holding up some photos. He tries to kick over a garbage can but, once again, can't muster the strength. Finally, someone takes pity on him and tips it over for him.

You see, once your eyes are opened to the message of Esse Quam Videri, you start to see it almost everywhere you look. Like no matter how much you may try to pass yourself off as the studly ladies' man who gets the girl...

Louie finds Vicky by the bar and taps her on the shoulder. "You know, there's nothing getting in our way now."

"I'm not following."

"Clear path. You and me. Getting together. All systems go."

"Yeah, I'm not so sure that's going to happen." She casts a glance over Louie's shoulder. Louie turns around and sees Niko standing there shrugging.

"What, how?" Louie blurts out.

Niko takes Louie for a stroll down memory lane to the scene where he and Louie arrive at the reunion. He tells Louie what he failed to notice was that Niko was standing directly behind Louie when he first spotted Vicky. As Niko describes it, Vicky sees Niko and lights up immediately. She holds his eye contact.

"It's you. I was hoping I'd see you here tonight."

Niko gives her his patented Niko wink and points to himself and her as if to say 'later, me and you.' Vicky nods and returns his wink.

...it's always the actual studly ladies' man who gets the girl.

Vicky consoles Louie by putting her hand on his shoulder. "So sorry, but I'm not interested."

"Dibs is relinquished," Niko triumphantly declares.

"If you knew this the whole time, why the deal making?"

"Because now I have the girl and the Tom Petty vinyl collection." With that, Niko puts his arms around Vicky and escorts her out.

Louie looks up and shouts at the heavens... "I HAD DIBS!"

***

Jeff and Ashley are walking down the main corridor of Holy Trinity looking at the different photos and decorations. They aren't saying anything; they're just silently enjoying the moment. Finally, a thought occurs to Ashley. "You just did something the old you wouldn't have done. Congratulations on taking the first step to becoming the new Jeff Dempsey."

Now it's Jeff who is struck by a sudden realization. He stops walking and turns to her. "Wait, you said before there were two things you did every day. The first is to do something the old you was too scared to do. What's the second one?"

"I make sure I give those experiences a voice by sharing them on my blog."

Jeff emphatically shakes his head. "I'm not really much of a writer."

Ashley considers it for a few seconds. "Even better."

Jeff sits in front of his computer in his bedroom as he works away on the webpage Myblog.com. He's to the point where he has to enter a name and, after some thought, begins typing 'Dempsey 2.0.'

He looks at it for a few seconds and makes a face. It's good but it's not perfect and so he deletes that title. He gives it more thought and is struck by a thought that makes his face light up. He eagerly types 'The New Twenty' and then sits back and smiles in satisfaction. He clicks a button that reads 'begin recording video blog' but when he looks up at the screen all he sees is black. "Son of a... Why can't I see anything?"

Somewhere in another part of the world, a 40-something-year-old man is scrolling through the myblog.com site when he comes to a link titled 'newest blogs' He sees one called *The New Twenty* and clicks on it. Jeff's face appears on his monitor.

So while I don't know precisely where this new adventure will take me, I'm okay with it.

Another man in his late 30's man is watching Jeff's vlog on his desktop PC.

Because while this particular yellow brick road might be scary and uncertain...

Three shirt-and-tie corporate types at a bar have also stumbled upon Jeff's vlog and watch it on a tablet.

...it also gives me a feeling of hope.

Tucked in her bed at home, Ashley is watching Jeff's vlog and smiling. In her hands is her copy of the high school yearbook from the year she was in the 10th Grade and Jeff graduated. She sets the yearbook down beside her and it falls open to the back inside cover where, hand drawn with a red pen is a heart and the initials G.H. + J.D. etched inside.

And you never know where that may lead.

Part Two

It Isn't Ironic

Tony Sekulich

CHAPTER FOUR

Two weeks have passed since Jeff's high school reunion, which no doubt will be remembered by his classmates simply as '*the incident,*' and he's still trying to figure out exactly what happened. At present, his head feels like a snow globe that has been firmly ensconced in a paint mixer for the better part of a day. It's cloudy, messy and will take a while for everything to settle. There's a fine line between a breakthrough and a breakdown and right now, it's anyone's guess as to which side of that line Jeff has landed.

Ashley's insistence that he undertake these bold new adventures and discuss them on a video blog had a certain appeal. Anything that frames him as bolder, more daring and less cowering under his bed like a puppy in a thunderstorm is certainly welcome. But like communism, hot yoga, and deep-fried Snickers bars, this might be another in the long list of things that are good only in theory.

And so, Jeff feels like he is at a crossroads as he sits and stares at his laptop's webcam. Much like a combatant sizing up his foe, he must decide to either engage or leave the battle for another day. With an all-too-familiar sigh of resignation, Jeff clicks the record button and his image appears on the screen.

I once asked a co-worker how his performance review went and he said, "They literally fucked me up the ass!" As my performance review was scheduled next, I was really hoping he simply misused the word 'literally.' Although I couldn't fight the curiosity as to how exactly a performance review would take that particular turn. 'Well Bill, you failed to meet your sales quota for the third straight quarter, I think you know what happens now.' I'll bet this happens more than we realize – misusing phrases, not employment-related sodomy. We toss around words and phrases without really understanding what they mean. Then one day we wake up to realize just how important these once seemingly abstract concepts can be in our lives. I recently had this kind of awakening which started, not surprisingly, in the bar with my friends.

At their regular table in the Cedar Room, Louie and Jeff sit with an almost trance-like fixation on something unfolding directly in front of them. At first glance, it's unclear if they are watching in silent judgment or are just completely engrossed in whatever is happening in front of them. Their concentration is such that they don't even notice when a completely exasperated Ashley plops herself down at the table.

"Anyone know where I can find a good caterer on short notice? Maybe one who won't back out just because his father needs a kidney." Had they been paying the slightest amount of attention, the guys would have picked up on the fact that Ashley used air quotes for 'needs a kidney'.

Jeff and Louie wave her off and shush her. "Niko's doing the thing again," Louie says, completely oblivious to the fact this raises more questions than it answers. Given Niko's rich history in the Cedar Room, this really isn't helpful information at all.

In a half-hearted attempt to clue her in, Jeff gestures with his head towards Niko who is sitting at a nearby table with Marlene, a stunningly beautiful mid-twenties woman with jet black hair and emerald green eyes.

Ashley now gets it. Whatever 'that thing' is, it is no doubt immature, boorish, and more than a little misogynistic. And yet, while her better angels call upon her to look away, lest she is even the slightest amount complicit in whatever awfulness Niko is currently undertaking, she finds herself unable. So while she is certain she will soon regret this, she scoots her chair a little closer to listen in to what Niko is saying.

"I remember how she left me on a stormy night. She kissed me and got out of our bed."

Niko delivers the words with the earnestness and sincerity of a deathbed confessional. Marlene is soaking all of it in. She squeezes his arm in a show of support.

"And though I pleaded and I begged her not to walk out that door..." he pauses to maintain his composure. "She packed her bags and turned right away."

"Oh, you poor thing."

"And she kept on telling me..." He's choking up now. He tries again. "She kept on telling me..." And again. "She kept on telling me I want you, I need you but...there ain't no way I'm ever gonna love you."

Marlene is close to heartbroken for him. She sighs audibly.

"No, don't be sad." Niko laughs through his mock pain. "Because two out of three ain't bad."

Marlene gives him a long comforting embrace. This would have been a tender and moving moment between two people sharing a real human connection if it weren't complete horseshit. And just as Ashley is certain she's seen rock bottom in male dating douchebaggery, Niko looks over to the gang and gives them a little wink. When Marlene goes up to the bar to get more drinks, Niko pulls his chair up to their table.

Ashley cannot hold her tongue. "You are such a lying pig!"

"Don't hate the player. Hate the overwrought yet haunting lyrics of one Jim Steinman. It's one of the advantages of dating younger women. They're mostly oblivious to all music BT."

Ashley turns to the others to see if this makes sense to them.

"Before Timberlake," Louie clarifies.

"Jeff, you gotta get in on this younger women action," Niko says.

Louie gets a certain look in his eye and swiftly removes himself from the table. He hurriedly makes his way to the bar.

"Yeah, I don't know if that's really for me," Jeff says in mild protest.

"What happened to taking on bold new adventures?" Niko presses. "Not once in your life have you dated outside your birth year. Get out there. Go meet a hot chick in her twenties."

Niko's advice had a ring of truth to it despite its obvious troubling implications. Once you blow past the 40 milestone, it's difficult to engage in a dating relationship with someone in their early 20's without being made to feel like a letch. Still, Niko knew whereof he spoke.

When they were back in Grade 11, Jeff refused to ask out a pretty Grade 10 student because he felt it would be unseemly to date someone younger. By the time he left university, he was married to Ellen but cast judgement on anyone who didn't follow the half-your-age-plus-seven guideline.

So this left him torn. Dating someone so young is not something he would normally be okay with. But isn't that exactly the point, he thought to himself. Isn't it his mission to do the things he wouldn't do before?

With that, Jeff turns to Ashley with a question in his eyes. She freezes. She knows exactly what the question is but she isn't sure how she should respond. Of course she wants him to take all necessary steps to becoming the new Jeff Dempsey. It's just that she never considered dating being one of them. When she rebuilt herself from her lowest point, everything she did was all about personal and spiritual self-improvement. It never occurred to her this would pop up on Jeff's radar.

And so what if it did? Why shouldn't he explore all options and who is she to say he shouldn't? So after what seems like an eternity... "While I can't condone the deception and misogyny of Niko's approach, I think it would be good for you get some practice in getting out of your comfort zone."

Jeff looks over and sees Katie, an attractive woman in her early twenties sitting at a table enjoying a book and a glass of red wine. Jeff gets up from the table and makes his way over to her.

"Can I just say that...yeah I might have chased a couple women around but all that ever got me was down. Then there those who made me feel good but never as good as I feel right now."

"Are you trying to pick me up with Tom Petty and the Heartbreakers lyrics?"

In the milliseconds after getting the last word out, Jeff pictured a hundred different responses she might come back with. In all of those possible scenarios, that was never one of them. Jeff is rocked back on his heels momentarily. "You know that song?"

"The Waiting, first track on side one off their 1981 album Hard Promises. No, never heard of it."

It's bad enough she tripped him up in his little ruse, but the sarcasm just feels like overkill. And yet, she has no shortage of sass which he can't help but find kind of sexy.

"Can I ask you something?" Katie continues. "Has that trick ever worked for you?" Her tone is more inquisitive than stern and admonishing. Jeff appears so inept at approaching women in bars that he has her genuinely curious.

"Well, this is the first time I've tried it so I'm guessing that answer is going to be no."

"For future reference, your ice-breaking skills are absolutely atrocious..."

Jeff nods in shame and is about to slink back to his table when Katie pushes out the chair opposite her.

"...but you have excellent taste in music."

Once again, the young woman catches Jeff by surprise. After a crash and burn of that magnitude, it is almost impossible to emerge from the wreckage unscathed. And yet, Jeff remarkably finds himself taking the seat across from her. He just stares into her eyes with a dumb grin on his face.

"This is where you should tell me your name," she says.

"Oh, right. I'm Jeff."

"Nice to meet you, Jeff. I'm Katie."

In the background, a woman at the bar slaps Louie across the face and dumps her drink over his head. Louie slowly walks back to his table where Niko cannot hide his smirk.

There could have been a million different things Louie could have said to the woman to elicit that reaction. But Niko doesn't have to play a guessing game. He knows Louie all too well by now. "You used *I Touch Myself* again didn't you?" Niko says.

"How are they not flattered by that?!?"

***

Minutes later, Niko walks out of the Cedar Room and begins the short walk back to his apartment. With plans already in place to see Marlene later that night, his work at the office is done for the day.

Or so he thought.

He's not 10 steps outside the door when he looks up and sees Tanya, a gorgeous blonde woman who appears distressed. She is on her phone and looking around for something. Niko sidles up beside her.

"You are way too pretty to look that distressed."

"I'm almost there, I gotta go." She smiles at Niko, "I'm looking for something."

"I think you found it."

"I'm looking for a place, actually. The Cedar Room."

Niko points to the Cedar Room sign behind her. "Like I said."

She looks behind her and smiles in embarrassment.

"Looks like the fates delivered you where you were supposed to be all along. Should we go inside and toast to the fates?"

"That's sweet. I'd love to but I'm here to meet someone for an appointment."

"Drinks another day then?"

"Wow, you're not short on confidence, are you? Does that usually work for you?" Unlike with Jeff and Katie, this question is more rhetorical. Tanya can already sense Niko is a bit of a player, but she feels an initial physical attraction. She knows damn well that approach usually works for him. As she's about to demonstrate.

"You tell me." Niko hands her his cell phone so she can enter her name and phone number.

She can't fight back a smile as she enters the info and hands it back to him.

"Tanya. I'm Nicholas." This is Niko's first rule about meeting someone brand new – never tell them the name you use on social media. A first meeting is not enough time to determine if someone is cuckoo for Cocoa Puffs. Until you know you'll want to see them more than once, use the practice Niko describes as 'name-adjacent'. A name which is similar to yours or a middle name. Something that can be explained away later but still serves as an effective smokescreen when they are trying to invite you to their sister's wedding after only one date.

He takes her hand in his. "Until we meet again." He kisses her hand.

***

On most days, apartment 9C at 325 Everwood Drive would not be considered presentable even under the most generous interpretation. This should not come as a complete surprise given it has recently become the domain of two single men in their 40's. In a plot point taken straight out *The Odd Couple*, ever since Jeff found himself single again, he has been living in his best friend's spare room. Of course, what the Neil Simon classic had that this situation does not is a Felix Unger. That's not to say that both Niko and Jeff are Oscars, they just don't make cleanliness their number one priority. They are more like Oscar-lites.

Of course, this is no ordinary day; this is Sunday brunch day. The tradition started some years back when the guys were in desperate need of a really good hangover cure. They felt that top quality eggs benedict and pancakes should not only be for women and gay men. Straight men should be able to enjoy a good Sunday brunch without judgmental gazes falling upon them. Of course, getting in to a good brunch place is near impossible on account of all the women and gay men so they decided to gather at Niko's.

The first step in the Sunday brunch routine is making sure the place is clean—genuinely clean. This has been most appreciated by Ashley, who has been a recent addition to the Sunday routine.

Jeff comes out from the kitchen carrying a piping hot quiche which he sets down on the middle of the dining room table. Niko is laying out the cutlery just as Ashley enters through the apartment door.

"Okay what floral arrangement goes best with a champagne and hot hors-d'oeuvres social?"

Jeff and Niko stare blankly at Ashley. It's essentially the same look she would have been met with had she asked, 'Who choreographed the 19th Century French Ballet 'La Bayadere'? The guys stood a better chance of coming up with the name Marius Petipa than naming the appropriate floral arrangement.

"This is one of those times when it sucks having all guy friends."

"You're welcome. It's our pleasure having you for brunch," Niko says with just enough sarcasm to make his point.

"Don't get your panties in a bunch. I'm having my annual gathering for my clients next week and everything needs to be perfect. I get most of my business from client referrals so if my clients are well fed and happy, my bank account is well fed and happy."

Louie enters the apartment. Niko looks over and sees Louie is empty-handed.

"And you don't have bagels because..."

"Oh shit! The bagels, I forgot. And why is it, by the way, I always have to bring the bagels. Is it because I'm Jewish?"

"You're a quarter Jewish and you've never stepped inside a Synagogue in your life. I'll tell you what, you can play the Jewish card when you can name one Book of the Old Testament."

Louie's brain starts whirring. "The Jungle Book?"

"Exactly. And to answer your question, it's because you live right next to the good bagel place. How could you forget in that short of a trip?"

"I ran into McNulty, you remember him from middle school? Anyway, we were chatting and catching up. It's ironic because I was wondering what was up to just the other day.

"Coincidental."

Louie is lost for a moment. "What?"

"You said ironic but you really meant coincidental."

Louie rolls his eyes. "Here we go with the grammar police."

"I'm not the grammar police," Niko protests.

He really is the grammar police. As a teacher, he considers himself the great defender of the Queen's English. What I've discovered is no matter how cool and aloof someone might be on the outside, deep inside everyone is a geek about something. Some may be punctuality geeks, others may be fact geeks, Niko is a grammar geek. He can't help himself. He will correct people's misuse of the language no matter the consequences.

Niko and Melanie, 31, a pretty brunette, are rolling around in bed.

"Oh my God. Oh, you are amazing. You've done this before, " he blurts out.

"What are you inferring, Niko? I'm not as innocent as you thought?"

Suddenly, Niko's' expression turns more serious.

"Implying."

"What?"

You said inferring but you meant implying. See since I'm the one who said it, I would be **implying** you are not innocent. And since you're the one who interpreted what I said, you would be **inferring** my meaning."

Melanie stops. "Are you correcting my grammar **while you're inside me**?"

"Is that a problem?"

"We're done here."

***

Jeff looks at his cell phone and makes a face. "What is going on with this girl? She's got me texting and every time I make a joke she writes back and says L-O-L. Why would she do that?"

Niko and Ashley exchange a look.

"So, are you two going to go out on a real date?" Ashley asks.

Niko jumps in before Jeff can answer, "That's not going to happen. This is Jeff Dempsey and he's going to let his hang-ups over their age difference bugger this thing up before it begins.

Jeff has taken jabs and ribbing from Niko before but there was something unsettling in what Niko just said. It was more than just playful teasing, it was an indictment of Jeff's character. In two sentences, Jeff was tried and convicted of having a major personality flaw. What bothers him more than the accusation is the realization that it's true.

Or rather, it was true. If Jeff is to become the man he always wanted to be, this is where change has to happen. With his eyes locked on Niko, Jeff picks up his cell phone and reads out loud as he texts.

"Meet you Friday at 8." Jeff looks up with a smug and satisfied look on his face. "There, was that the action of someone who's going to bugger this up?"

Niko's phone buzzes indicating an incoming text message. Jeff's look of concern and Niko's smug look shows that both know exactly what happened. And while no words need to be said, Niko just can't let the moment pass. He shows Jeff his phone. "You just sent that to me so I'll let you answer that."

***

Jeff sits alone at a small table for two in a quiet dessert cafe. He is staring at the front door and occasionally glances at his watch.

Jeff's cell phone buzzes indicating a text message. He looks at it and sees a series of three emojis. There is a man running, a clock, and the sad face. A second text comes right after it which reads, 'WAN2 meet @ * $ instead?'

If Jeff had an emoji to English dictionary, he would understand that she was saying 'I'm running late and this makes me sad. Do you want to meet at Starbucks instead?' Without the translation, Jeff is lost and confused. He looks at it like it's Mandarin. He then responds: *No problem, sounds good.*

Katie responds: 'BCNU B4N' followed by a smiley face. This means 'I'll be seeing you. Bye for now.'

Again, Jeff had no idea what she as saying but the presence of the smiley face at the end has to be a good sign, he figured.

Thirty minutes later, Jeff impatiently fidgets with the silverware. His cell phone buzzes again with another TM. It reads: WRU@.

Even someone with Jeff's novice emoji abilities should be able to figure this one means 'Where are you at?'. Sadly, he cannot. Jeff responds: *Where are you?*

Katie responds by texting three coffee cup icons.

The coffee cup icons did not tip Jeff off that they were clearly on different pages. Jeff responds: Are you coming soon? How long should I wait?

Katie responds: WRU@???? This is quickly followed by three crying-face emojis.

By this point Jeff had given up trying to decipher the messages. This could explain why he was not at all concerned by the three emojis indicating weariness and distress. Naturally, Katie was only further confused by his response. 'Okay, I'll wait here a little longer.'

Katie has now abandoned all playfulness and texting politeness. Her exasperation is in the driver's seat: 'WTF????'

Jeff has also reached the tipping point of impatience with this exchange. He looks around and sees a couple out for dessert with their two teenage daughters. There comes a point when frustration and desperation give us blinders to our actions. Our laser focus on a desire to accomplish a certain goal renders us unable to see how the action may be perceived by others. Jeff will later use this explanation for what he is about to do next.

"I'm terribly sorry to interrupt your dessert, I was just wondering if I might be able to borrow one of your daughters for just a bit?"

"Excuse me?"

"They're both fairly young so either one will do."

"What the hell do you think you're doing?"

"Oh no, no, no. Don't get the wrong idea. I just want to show them something on my phone."

The next thing Jeff knows, he is being escorted out by a burly waiter and shoved out on the street. Jeff screams inside through the closed door.

"I just want to know - what the fuck does WTF mean?!?"

***

The lights in the apartment have been turned down to cruising level as Niko and Tanya sit together on the sofa. This is Niko in his natural habitat. He gives her the thousand-watt smile as he tops up her glass of red wine.

"If I didn't know better, I'd say you were trying to get me drunk."

Niko feigns shock. "Why would you think that?"

"It's just my pattern with men. I always seem drawn to the alpha male types who just want to get me into bed and then never call again."

"Men can be such jerks."

"But I'm seeing somebody about it and she's helping me establish boundaries. You know, if this were before I started my sessions with her, we'd already be in your bedroom right now."

"Really?"

"Oh yeah. I would have felt the need to win your affection by giving in to your every dark and twisted sexual desire."

Niko is in actual pain now. He does his best to conceal his agony.

"But it's like she always says about the bad boys - if you give in to the heat, you'll end up getting burned."

"Well, I don't see any bad boys here tonight. Do you?"

"No."

And there it is – the green light Niko has been waiting for. It's the international signal for 'enough chit-chat, let's take this evening to the next level'. Accordingly, Niko scoots over a little closer to her.

"It's just me and you..."

At that precise moment, Jeff comes barging in through the apartment door.

"...and my roommate Jeff."

"That was a total disaster. Did you ever have a night with such high hopes that just imploded in a colossal way?"

Whatever romantic vibe Niko had so carefully crafted has disappeared in a flash. Tanya feels it immediately.

"I should probably get going," she offers.

"Yeah, I think I can picture it," Niko says coldly. He walks Tanya to the door.

"Maybe we can pick up where we left off another night."

"I'd like that."

Niko smiles as he closes the door then spins around on Jeff. "Thank you for that."

Jeff all but ignores that last comment. In his defense, he didn't really hear it. Jeff is experiencing a rage-induced narcissism that renders him oblivious to everything around him. He can't see anything that's not related to his current predicament.

"I don't know if I can date these younger women. They communicate almost entirely in happy faces and unintelligible writing. For the life of me, I can't understand any of it.

"Give me your phone."

Jeff hands him his cell phone and Niko starts working away on it.

"Looks like I have to Jeff-proof this for you."

"We tried to meet up but we just couldn't connect. She's going to think I'm either a jerk or an idiot."

"Most likely, both," Niko says.

Niko hands Jeff's phone back to him. It starts buzzing then a robotic female voice starts speaking from the phone.

'New text message from Niko. Message. This program will translate and read out all of your text messages and emojis. Laughing out loud. Smiley Face.'

Jeff looks on in amazement.

"Laughing out loud! Who could possibly have known that?"

The phone buzzes again. "Text from Niko - Embarrassed face."

"Jeff proof."

***

The following evening Louie, Niko, and Ashley sit at their usual Cedar room table. Louie looks at his watch.

"It's ironic. Jeff's usually the first one here."

Niko has heard enough, he can't take any more. The grammar police are out in full force and looking to bust heads. "For the love all that is Holy and Sacred, that doesn't make it ironic. That makes it unusual. For something to be ironic, the outcome has to mock the intent."

"Well, then I still don't get it."

"An Oracle tells Oedipus he will kill his father and marry his mother. This freaks him out so much he flees his hometown. Along this new journey, he kills someone who he thinks is a stranger. This turns out to be his father and the ensuing chain of events leads to him marrying his mother, although he doesn't know it at the time. The act of fleeing his hometown was supposed to prevent this horrible fate from happening but instead, it is what caused it. That is ironic."

Louie stares at him blankly for a few seconds. "That's just sick!"

Jeff arrives and sits down at the table but his body language is dejected and defeated.

"What's the matter with you?" Ashley asks.

"I may have blown it with Katie."

"I'm sure it's not as bad as you think."

"OK, so you know how Katie and I have been texting back-and-forth? That's the only way we communicate and the other day, I dropped my phone in the tub. So I had to do the bag of rice thing and I was without my phone for a couple of days. And then I realized, if she sent me some text, she's going to think I'm not responding to her or I'm just blowing her off. So I had to find a way to get a hold of her.

"So you just left her a Facebook message?" Ashley says hopefully.

"I would have done that but we're not Facebook friends so I just went and googled her name and found out that she had posted to a violinist online group."

"Please tell me that's all you did," Niko says.

"Well, I figured I would just leave her a message on the message board or maybe I could, you know, send her a direct message. But as it turns out, you can't message somebody in this group unless you yourself are a member."

Niko continues to be horrified. "Oh no, please tell me you didn't..."

"I joined the group as a member just so I could send her a message and explain. So I said, 'Hey I dropped my phone in some water. If you're trying to get a hold of me, I'm not blowing you off.'"

"So you cyber-stalked her?" Ashley clarifies.

"No, I used basic online investigative techniques to track her down, find out a private club she's a part of and then I posed as a member of that club and contacted her..." Jeff stops, a light has just gone on for him. "Oh, okay, I see it now. Yeah, I cyber-stalked her."

"I think you should sit in on a session with my client when we talk about boundaries. Ashley looks up and sees the client coming through the door. "And there she is now." Ashley gets up and goes over to greet her client.

"Don't worry buddy. We're not going anywhere until we figure this out."

Niko looks up and sees Ashley with her client, which turns out to be Tanya. His face goes white. He stands up.

"Okay, we're outta here."

"What happened to no-"

Niko grabs Jeff by the arms and starts pulling him along. "Shut up and move your ass!"

CHAPTER FIVE

Back in the safety of their apartment, the gravity of Jeff's situation is beginning to settle in with him. Someone showing dogged persistence is endearing, even admirable. However, just millimeters beyond dogged persistence is where Jeff now resides – certified cyberstalker. And even a technophobe like him can see that's a hard place to come back from. These are the thoughts that consume him as he paces the living room floor as a bemused Niko looks on.

"I have to do something," Jeff finally blurts out.

"You have to do nothing. You won't last ten minutes out there until you learn the secret to dating younger women."

Jeff stops pacing.

"Do not come off as needy. This is an absolute. It must be obeyed. Like never feeding Gremlins after midnight."

Jeff's cell phone beeps, he looks and his face lights up.

"I kind of feel like that ship has sai-" the buzzing of his cell phone stops him mid-sentence. He eagerly fishes the phone out his pants pocket. "It's Katie."

Niko lunges and grabs the cell phone out of Jeff's hand. "It's time for lesson number one of the do-not-be-needy playbook. Wait one hour before replying to texts, unless it's a weekend night in which case don't text back until the next day."

"That's crazy."

"If you're dating a 38-year-old, it's okay to respond right away. But a 21-year-old reacts to desperation like a Gremlin reacts to water."

"What's with th-"

"It was on the movie channel last night. Phoebe Cates."

"Nice!"

***

Later that night in Ashley's condo, she finds herself on the edge of her sofa with a perplexed look on her face. "You want my advice?" she asks in complete disbelief.

The question is neither rhetorical nor to herself. She is genuinely interested in the reason Niko has come to her in search of life advice. There are several things she would have considered more likely happening to her that night. Included in that list are a polar bear attack, being serenaded by Justin Beiber, and being serenaded in a duet by Justin Beiber and a polar bear.

"It's my little cousin," Niko offers. "She has a history of going from one bad boy to the next and she keeps getting her heart broken. I just wish I could help her."

Ashley is naturally inclined to be suspicious of Niko. His virtuoso performance of the Meatloaf song earlier has not been forgotten. But if he has come to her in a sincere call for help, she can't really turn him away. Hearing his story, it sounds fairly plausible so she decides to proceed with caution.

"Women with self-esteem issues look for the shortest route to validation. That almost always means sex. You have to tell your cousin that she needs to take it slow and find her validation in the little parts of building the relationship. I'll often tell my clients - when it comes to the bad boys, if you give in to the heat, you'll end up getting burned."

"Such great, great advice. But won't these guys try to work around that?"

"Probably."

"How specifically would they go about working around that. You know, just so I can inform her." As nonchalantly as he can, Niko pulls and notepad and a pen out of his jacket pocket.

"Well, the smart ones will find a way to undermine her self-esteem. Find little ways to make her insecure, thus driving up her need for instant validation."

Niko starts jotting this down. "Oh, that's great. Really good stuff."

Ashley shoots him a concerned look.

"Good stuff to help my cousin," he quickly clarifies. "Keep going."

***

So while Niko was building his own playbook, I was out with Katie and a few of her friends. Luckily I was able to convince her I'm not a cyber-stalker and so she invited me to meet some of her friends at one of their favorite hang-outs. I still had Niko's words in my head on his don't-come-off-as-needy strategy.

If you're out with a younger woman at the bar, leave her for 30-minute stretches of time to flirt with other girls. If she sees three or more girls laughing along with you, you score bonus points.

At a break in the group conversation at the table, Jeff excuses himself and steps away from Katie and her friends. He scans the bar and sees another table of young women just across the bar. Their laughter and table full of empty drink glasses lead Jeff to conclude they are an excellent target for the next part of his plan. He goes over and approaches an attractive brunette.

"So what's the worst opening line someone's used on you?"

The brunette looks him up and down with contempt.

"That one."

Jeff peaks over his shoulder and catches Katie looking at him. Jeff breaks out into an over-the-top fake laugh.

Jeff hoped the next attempt would prove to be less humiliating. It was not. In fact, it seemed to get worse with each unsuccessful attempt to impress a table full of young women. Among his ill-conceived tactics included card tricks, doing the robot, and a mediocre Austin Powers impression. In the process, he lost track of both time and his date for the night. When Jeff returns to Katie's table. He finds she isn't there anymore.

I learned two things that night. One – there's a shelf life to the adorableness of the phrase, 'Do I make you horny, baby.'

Katie's friend simply points towards the door.

And when it comes to playing the dating games, sometimes you can be too clever for your own good.

***

Niko and Tanya are alone again in the apartment but this time, Niko's not putting on the full court press.

"I really appreciate that you're willing to take it slow. You're not like the rest of the guys."

"Yeah a lot of my friends are hung up on women with like perfect bodies but I'd rather be with someone like you."

The off-hand comment was like a surgical strike that hits its mark. Tanya is clearly insulted and motivated to rebut.

"I have a great body!"

"No, of course. What's great about it is that it's real. It's not one of those perfect lingerie model bodies. It's your imperfections that make you perfect just the way you are." His last few words hang in the air with their condescending and patronizing putrid stench.

"Imperfections?!? Are you kidding me? I work out every day and do yoga three times a week. I defy you to find one single imperfection on this body."

Tanya stands up and starts unbuttoning her top. She only gets two buttons in when Jeff comes barreling through the apartment door bringing her to a sudden halt.

"Your plan didn't work!"

Niko collapses back on the sofa in agony. "You've got to be kidding me!"

Once again, Tanya senses the mood is ruined and quickly excuses herself. She is out of the apartment in a flash.

"Any other brilliant ideas?" Jeff offers, still oblivious to what he has done.

Niko gives it a few second's thought. "We could always go French Renaissance on her ass."

***

Miraculously, Jeff was able to convince Katie to join him for a quiet, let-me-make-it-up-to-you date at a *Nuit Blanche*, a fancy French restaurant. Jeff and Katie are bathed in candlelight as they raise a glass in a toast.

"This is really nice," she says. "I have to say, you had me worried after the other night."

"Yeah, that was not one of my finer moments. But if you think about it, it was kind of your fault."

"Really? And why is that?"

Jeff pauses for a moment.

"Because in every man's heart there is a secret nerve that answers to the vibrations of beauty."

Yes, I was that smooth. Though to be fair, I had a little help. Niko's idea to go French Renaissance involved launching a plan we called "Operation Cyrano.

The dimly lit setting is no accident. It was chosen so it would be easier for Niko to remain unnoticed as he sat within earshot of their conversation. Specifically, he is seated behind a post next to their table but out of her eye line. Niko feeding Jeff lines on the instant messaging program on his smartphone. Jeff is listening to the robotic voice reading his text messages through a tiny Bluetooth earbud which Katie has yet to notice.

Just like in the play, it was a huge success. I was going with whatever Niko was feeding me and it all worked beautifully. And the reason it worked in the play was because Cyrano was giving Christian and Roxanne his undivided attention. What Cyrano was not doing was sexting with the hot blonde he was trying to bang.

"My mom wants to come visit soon but I'm not sure how I feel about that," Katie explains. "Sometimes she can be difficult to be around."

Niko sees a message come through from Tanya It reads "I'm feeling a little naughty right now." This excites Niko so much, he ends up dropping the phone and when he picks it up, he doesn't realize he's switched chat conversations. He starts typing.

Because the plan has worked so well this far, Jeff decides to trust whatever Niko sends him. Which is why his response to Katie is...

"Such a dirty girl!"

Katie is a bit confused. Jeff presses on.

"Sounds like someone is in desperate need of a good spanking."

Katie is really thrown by this.

"What?!?"

"You know what I'm going to do with that dirty girl? I'm going to..."

Let's just say the completion of that thought was not exactly restaurant appropriate.

Katie stands up and steps up to a cowering Jeff.

"Don't call me ever again!"

She storms off and Jeff peaks around the corner to glare at a contrite Niko who offers a 'mea culpa' shrug. Jeff's cell phone beeps with one more message.

Sux 2 B U.

CHAPTER SIX

Desperate, lost, and frantic, Jeff finds himself in the same place he usually does in the situations, at the Cedar Room with his friends. After suffering the biggest humiliation to date, Jeff is desperate to make amends with Katie but can't think of a good way to do it. It's not like Hallmark has a card that says, 'I'm sorry I mistakenly offered to gratify your mother sexually. I hope we can still be friends'.

Niko and Louie were also there with him and could tell Jeff was getting lost in a thought spiral. They've seen this many times before, Jeff gets lost in his own thoughts and he may as well be 1,000,000 miles away. It was time to snap him out of it.

"Just go to her and tell her what happened," Niko said matter-of-factly.

"I don't know where to find her and even if I did, I wouldn't even know what to say."

"She should be a breeze to find," Louie said. "Women that age are always talking about where they are and what they're doing. Just go on her social media."

"Yeah, because that's worked so well for him before," Niko says.

Just then, Ashley comes in and plops down at the table. "I'm so screwed. My wait staff canceled for my champagne social tomorrow night. Get this - they're actors who just got hired for the same production. Leave it to me to hire the only two actors in this city who can actually find work."

"What about me?" Louie asks.

"You have a full-time job and don't pay rent."

"So what. I like cash."

"Okay fine. You're lucky I'm desperate."

Niko's cell phone rings. The call display shows it's Tanya.

"Well hello there."

"Hi. I only have a minute but I was wondering if you wanted to be my date to my life coach's party tomorrow night."

Niko did his best to conceal that he was immediately overcome with terror. He had yet to seal the deal with Tanya and he knew that if Ashley knew they were secretly seeing each other, she would put the kibosh on it before he could experience the sheer euphoria of that first unhooked bra clasp. No, he thought to himself, it cannot end here.

"Couldn't we just meet up after it?" he offered.

"I was telling her about you today and she said if you were really different from the other jerks, you'd come with me to important functions. She said if you don't come with me, it will prove you're just trying to get into my pants."

Niko is now glaring at Ashley. "She said that? Well, of course, I'll come with you. Is it okay if I meet you there?"

"Sure."

"Great. Can't wait. Okay, bye."

Niko hangs up.

"I'm so screwed."

***

Later that night when Jeff should have been sleeping, he instead found himself in front of his computer pouring through Katie's social media pages. As he scrolls through updates, he sees one from earlier that day that reads. 'Can't wait to lead the mob squad tonight at Dorchester Square.'

There's a part of him that thought for a second, 'You realize every other time you've tried this it's ended up in abject failure and humiliation.' But like all the other times, he convinced himself this time it'll be better. Jeff is like a degenerate gambler in Vegas. He's convinced that yes, he's left his money at the casino all that all those other times but now he has a sure-fire system to win it all back.

***

Ashley is attending to the flowers and the decorations when her doorbell rings. She answers the door to find a very spiffy Louie done up in classy black and white with some grocery bags in his arms.

"Nice duds!"

"Hey, I am nothing if not all class."

"Well, at least half that sentence is true." She is cross-checking their bags with the list.

"Did you bring the ice?"

There is a prolonged silence. Louie looks down at his shoes.

"Louie! Is this the bagel incident all over again?"

Louie just shrugs.

"I've got 45 people coming over for champagne and no ice to chill it? My whole next year depends on this night. It has to go off with exact precision. I need you to go out and get ice now!"

Ashley takes the bags inside to continue her preparation as Louie starts towards the building's front door. Suddenly Niko appears panting and gasping from what was a dead sprint from his apartment to Ashely's. Niko is the fittest and most athletic of the group, but that run has kicked his ass and it shows. What's even odder than the fact that he sprinted to Ashley's is the attire he did it in. He's dressed in what is commonly known as business casual with a blue button-down shirt and gray cotton pants. The unquestionable highlight of the ensemble is what appears to be a brand-new brown suede jacket.

"New jacket! Someone's trying to impress," Louie says playfully. Niko appears in no mood for games.

"This is not just a *new jacket*, this is tan calf suede with 100% genuine leather body lining and brown ribbed trims. It cost me a fortune but it will all be worth it when I'm putting Tanya in a cab at four o'clock in the morning. Is Ashley here?"

"She's in her condo."

Niko steps closer to Louie and speaks in a hushed tone.

"Okay here's the thing – tonight you are my wingman. There will be a very hot blonde showing up soon. Under no circumstances are she and I and Ashley to be in the same place at the same time. Any two are fine but if you see the third coming, throw your body in front of her."

"You got it."

Louie starts for the front door.

"Where are you going?" Niko asks incredulously. "She could show up any moment now."

"I need to go for ice."

"Not right now, you're not. Figure something out."

"No, I <u>have to</u> get ice. Ashley's going to kill me because I forgot to bring it when I showed up."

"Was it the bagel incident all over again?"

"Why won't you people let that go?!?"

"Just stay here and help me out," Niko pleads. "I promise I'll help you figure out something with the ice, okay?"

Before Louie can answer, Ashley opens the front door and is more than a little surprised to see Niko there. In all of his planning to keep Ashley and Tanya apart, he neglected to come up with a legitimate reason for being there. He can't tell her that he's the plus-one for one of her invited guests. Fortunately for him, this is not the first time he's had to think on his feet when bending the truth. "Oh, that's right, this is your party night, isn't it?"

"Yeah. What are you doing here?"

"I just popped by to say thank you for helping me with my cousin. She's doing much better now. Heck, I'm almost a client myself now. Maybe I should stick around for a bit tonight."

Ashley can't tell if that's purely a joke or if he's genuinely hinting that he'd like to stick around. In either case, she can't think of what harm could come from his staying. "If you want."

After a few more moments of awkward silence, Ashley goes back into her condo while Niko exhales in relief.

***

Jeff wanders through Dorchester square looking around until he finally spots Katie who is hanging out on a park bench. He starts walking towards her and when she looks up and spots him. Jeff can see the concern written all over her face. And really, who could blame her? For a guy who's desperate to make the case he's not a cyber-stalker, showing up unannounced to the place she mentioned she'd be on her social media posts is a move ill-conceived at best. Each desperate attempt to convince her he's not a creep is only doing him a disservice. He's banking on this last-ditch attempt turning the tide. For that to happen, he's going to have to find a way to get her to listen with an open mind. This in itself could generously be considered a longshot.

"I know you said you didn't want to see me, but I had to talk to you," Jeff pleads.

"There's nothing to talk about."

"I can't let it go until I've had the chance to explain."

Slowly people start gathering around the area where Katie has been waiting. Of course, being totally wrapped up in his own thing right now, Jeff doesn't notice.

"Jeff, I can't do this right now," she says.

"It never seems like the right time to allow yourself to take a chance. You just have to do it."

Katie steps up to him and speaks slowly punctuating the key words with her cadence.

"You're not hearing me. I can't do this...right now!"

***

Niko and Ashley are chatting in a corner of the condo when he sees Tanya enter. Niko kicks Louie who is right beside him and gestures with his head that Tanya is the one to look out for. Tanya sees Niko and Ashley in the corner, starts waving frantically and starts over towards them.

Niko instinctively starts doing the fake cough thing, which is supposed to be inconspicuous although anybody who's ever seen it and practice knows it is anything but. "Code red! Code red!"

Louie leaps into action and jumps directly in front of Tanya's path. He grabs her by the arms and escorts in the other direction.

"Excuse me, Miss. Could you come with me please?"

He leads her to the back hallway.

As she is being led down the main hallway she is more confused than concerned. It's always startling when a strange man inexplicably jumps in your path and starts escorting you in a new direction. That said, very few attackers greet their victims with 'excuse me, miss' and, as odd as Louie can come across, there is an unmistakable harmless quality about him. "What do you want?" she asks with earnest curiosity.

"I need your help with..."

He glances all over his immediate surroundings like a pudgier Keyser Soze and spots the fire extinguisher hanging on the wall.

"Fire...."

"... safety," Niko ads as he enters the picture.

"Fire safety?" Tanya asks incredulously.

"It's my responsibility to test the fire safety equipment and I need a party guest to be part of it so they know we didn't fudge the results," Louie explains.

Louie grabs the extinguisher and hands it to Tanya and he sneaks a peek to see where Ashley is.

"So just give this a blast and we'll see how it goes," Niko says.

Tanya squeezes the handle and a blast of FREEZING cold Co2 hits Niko on the hand.

Ashley turns the corner and Niko quickly pulled Tanya into a spare bedroom. Ashley sees Louie holding the fire extinguisher and is more than little confused.

"What are you doing back here? And where are we on the chilled champagne? I can't stall people much longer."

"Almost ready. Real close."

Ashley goes back to her guests and Niko reappears as Tanya joins the other guests.

"Holy crap that blast is cold." Suddenly his face changes expression. "That blast of Co2 is freezing cold!"

Louie just stares at him blankly. He has no idea where Niko is going with this. Niko grins from ear to ear. "Louie, my friend I think I just solved our champagne-chilling dilemma."

***

Jeff remains determined to get through to Katie and even though she seems preoccupied with whatever is going on at the Square, he refuses to give up. Katie walks away from Jeff but he stays with her in lockstep. Katie gets to the middle of the square and stops.

"I have been in and out of terrible relationships since I was sixteen. I spent two decades believing that being in a relationship is about obligations and chores. And I didn't know it could be any other way until I met you."

Katie's facial expression gives away her dismay. With just a word, she is pleading for him to stop. "Jeff!"

Suddenly music starts playing over a public sound system. Any hope she had that the music would deter Jeff from continuing are immediately dashed when he resorts to shouting over the music.

"And from that first moment we started spending time together, I knew we could have something special. I was so terrified you would never go for a guy over 40, I just did whatever I thought would keep you from losing interest."

Suddenly and inexplicably, Katie starts into a dance routine. Jeff is a bit perplexed but carries on.

"It's not easy being 40 and out there again on the dating scene. Almost everyone else your age is settled with the wife and 2.5 perfect kids and the house in the suburbs. It's like the whole world is moving in one direction and you're moving in the other. Do you have any idea what that feels like?"

Amongst the countless things in his immediate area that Jeff doesn't see are the other people in the square directly behind him dancing in perfect sync with Katie. Once again, Jeff's temporary narcissistic blinders are in full effect.

***

Niko and Louie have locked themselves in the bathroom. They have a couple of champagne bottles in the tub as Niko stands over them with the fire extinguisher. He is about to blast them when he suddenly puts the extinguisher down and starts taking off his jacket. He hands to jacket to Louie who is standing by the door.

"Can't let anything happen to this. Go put it in another room."

Louie ducks out of the room as Niko turns his head and unloads on the bottles. After a good 30 second blast, he grabs a towel and wipes the foam off the bottles. Louie comes back in and Niko looks at him and smiles.

"They're cold?" Louie asks tentatively

"They're cold!"

"Niko pops open the bottles and starts filling champagne glasses on the tray on the bathroom countertop. "I am a Golden God! Lou, I have the feeling we're going to be talking about this for a long time to come!"

***

Jeff is watching as Katie is busting out full-on dance moves. Jeff stands there looking on, still unaware he is caught in the middle of a flash mob.

"You can dance all you want, I'm not going away until you talk to me."

"Turn around Jeff."

"I'm not leaving."

"I'm not asking you to leave. I'm asking you to turn around."

Jeff turns around and sees that more than one hundred people are all dancing in sync and he is caught at the front of it.

"You wanna talk, we'll talk but you gotta do something for me first. You gotta dance!"

Jeff tries dancing along with everyone else but it is a complete disaster. He trips over himself and stumbles into people behind him. They shove him off and he stumbles onto other people to his right. They shove him into other dancers and the disruption starts to snowball. Jeff tries to escape but only winds up knocking down more dancers back in the pack. As public disasters go, this one is spectacular.

***

Louie carries a tray of glasses filled with cold champagne. He catches Ashley's eye who gives him an approving nod. Louie goes over to Niko and Tanya.

"How's the avoiding going?" Louie whispers to Niko.

"Up til now, pretty good. But I need you to be on constant alert."

"Hey, guys."

Louie turns around and is horrified to see Ashley has joined the group.

"Or that could happen," Niko says to Louie in a hushed but stern tone.

They all stand there quietly exchanging glances. Niko is too terrified to say anything. At this point, he's wondering if he could survive the fourth-floor fall because, at that particular moment, leaping off the balcony seems like the best of all options. Louie is thinking of how he's going to explain to Niko that he failed in the only job he was given that night and is wondering exactly how Niko will punish him and for how long. Finally, it's Ashley who breaks the awkward silence.

"I wouldn't waste your time on this one," she says to Niko. "She's got a new boyfriend."

Tanya laughs thinking Ashley has made an obvious joke. Niko seizes on the opportunity and laughs louder than the others. Louie seizes on his opportunity to escape retribution from Niko and starts pulling Ashley towards the kitchen.

"Ashley, can I talk to you for a moment?"

Tanya turns to Niko and smiles. "I really want to thank you for coming tonight. I think it's time that we took this to the next level," she says with more than a hint of playfulness in her voice.

Upon hearing the last bit, Niko takes a step back and bumps into a guy pouring himself a drink. The guy drops the bottle of 150 proof liquor and it smashes on the floor with most of the splash covering Niko's pants. While people rush over to help clean up the mess, Tanya leans into Niko.

"Why don't we get you out of these wet clothes."

She starts towards the spare bedroom as she gives him the come-hither finger. Niko can't believe his good fortune. He went from disaster to ecstasy in about 45 seconds and all it took was a pair of wet pants.

"Here? Now? Oh yeah!"

***

Jeff and Katie sit on the edge of the public fountain. Jeff is tending to some bumps and bruises. "I'm sorry I screwed everything up."

"They'll get over it."

A woman walks by stops in front Jeff. "Thanks a lot, asshole!"

"Eventually," Katie adds.

"I meant I'm sorry I messed everything up with you."

From the time he approached her in the bar, this feels like the first honest sentiment he's expressed to her. This long-overdue show of honesty is what prompts her to respond in kind. "You think I didn't know what you were doing the whole time? The waiting an hour to return texts, chatting up other girls in the bar. All these guys my age are reading from the same playbook and I'm sooooooo tired of that scene. The reason I wanted to spend time with you was because I thought finally, here's a guy who's past all that game playing bullshit."

And that's when my great awakening overtook me. Right then, I realized that irony was more than just a misunderstood phrase overused by today's millennials. It was also the universe's way of punctuating teachable moments in life. Like even though you may be twice as old as the person you're dating...

Katie takes Jeff's hand and looks deep into his eyes. "I'm willing to give this a shot, but you're going to have to drop these immature games and, well...act your age."

...you're the one who has to grow up.

***

Niko and Tanya have snuck off to Ashley's spare bedroom where they have lit some candles and are well on their way to having sex on her bed. Niko's pants are around his ankles and, in all the commotion, they don't notice when a candle falls off the dresser and on to the floor right next to Niko's feet.

Or it could teach you that sometimes when you give in to the heat...

A small orange glow can be seen behind Niko who stops what he's doing and looks around.

"Is that...fire?" Niko asks.

"Oh yeah baby, we're on fire," Tanya whispers.

Niko gets up and notices that his pants, bunched around his ankles, are completely engulfed in flames.

...it's the bad boy who ends up getting burned.

Niko tries to run but trips himself and falls on the floor.

Bonus points if the liar <u>literally</u> has his pants on fire.

"Put me out! Put me out!"

The loud thud of Niko hitting the hardwood floor could be heard and felt throughout the rest of Ashley's apartment. A combination of concern and curiosity sent a herd of party guests charging into the room with Ashley leading the pack. As she comes barging through the door, she is stopped by the sight of Niko writhing around on her bedroom floor, his pants around his ankles and engulfed in flames.

"Somebody get the fire extinguisher!" Ashley calls out as she tries stomping out the flames.

"Nicholas? Are you okay?" Tanya says.

"This is Nicholas?" It's amazing how fast someone can go from genuine concern to seething rage. In this case, it took about the length of time it takes Ashley to raise her foot and bring it back down again. In an instant, she goes from stomping out the flames to aggressively stomping on Niko.

Louie comes charging in with a fire extinguisher. "I have the extinguisher but..."

"Louie, blast the damn thing!" Ashley screams. "Preferably in his face!"

Louie tries to blast Niko with the extinguisher but nothing comes out. Ashley quickly scans the room and spots Niko's suede jacket which his hanging on a hook on the bedroom door. She grabs it and uses it to smother the flames.

"Not the jacket!" Niko shouts.

With similar aggression, Ashley beats out the flames while getting a few good whacks in on Niko. When she's done, Ashley holds up the coat which is burned beyond salvation.

Or it can be as simple as the precise moment when the student schools the master.

"Wait, I get it," Louie exclaims. "You didn't want your precious jacket to get damaged by the fire extinguisher so you had me put it in this room. But because I put it in this room and you used up the fire extinguisher, it got ruined in a fire. That's ironic."

Niko just looks at him with contempt.

"Wonderful, now you get it!"

And lastly, it can explain how a guy who ruined an attempt at creating an internet viral video...

Jeff brings up YouTube and clicks on a video called, 'Idiot ruins flashmob.' The video shows Jeff getting in the way of the emerging flashmob in the square. It shows how the group quickly went from flash mob to angry mob as they turn on Jeff and start beating and kicking him.

Is the latest viral sensation with over four hundred thousand hits today. Ironic...isn't it?

Tony Sekulich

Part Three

The Luke & Leia Moment

Tony Sekulich

CHAPTER SEVEN

It's been two months to the day since 'Extreme Makeover: Jeff Edition' started and when pondering this fact, Jeff feels a little uneasy. Partially because he believes celebrating 'monthiversaries' should be relegated to couples under the age of 18. There's nothing quite as sad as middle-aged men and women excited because they are going out to celebrate their four-month anniversary. Except maybe those who don't even have four month anniversaries but that's still debatable.

The other reason Jeff feels uneasy is because he knows anytime he's tried something new, this is about the time he's bailed. CrossFit lasted 57 days which was 55 days after he became convinced it should be categorized as a cult. Art classes lasted 61 days, while Thai Fusion cooking classes set the high-water mark at a whopping 68 days.

So while he is a little concerned he might slip back to his old ways, he also has to admit that he isn't hating his new life. He and Katie, after what could generously be called a rocky start, have been going strong for six weeks. What do you get somebody for a six-week anniversary, Jeff thought to himself. That's right, nothing because it's not a real thing.

Even the weekly blogging was getting easier and easier for him. He no longer stares at the webcam with dread and apprehension. And even he would have to admit that he was getting better at it. One might even say he was enjoying it.

Case in point – Jeff walks into his bedroom, flips open his computer, fires up the webcam and launches into a new post.

When I was a kid, my grandmother had this framed picture that always bothered me. It was one of those optical illusions where it was a picture of a haggard old woman or a pretty young girl, depending on how you saw it. I don't know why it creeped me out so much. I guess it made me uncomfortable that it wasn't one thing or another. Maybe that's why every time I looked at it, all I could see was the old woman. I thought of that picture this past weekend. Our old college friend Hillary's wedding was fast approaching. We were all invited but...

"I'm out," Louie declares emphatically. Louie always had a flair for the dramatic and was never one to pass up the opportunity to make an entrance. On this occasion, his grand entrance takes place at their regular table in the Cedar Room. Niko, Ashley, and Jeff are already there for their regular Friday after work drinks gathering.

It used to be a regular thing for a larger group when they were all in their early to mid-twenties. But as people started having kids and moving out to the suburbs, the regular thing became more and more irregular. Despite not having kids or moving to the suburbs, Jeff was one of the first ones to drop off. Ellen didn't see the point in a married man hanging out in bars.

So as odd as it may seem, getting back to the old routine was a key step in Jeff forging his new path.

"Out? Out of what?" Jeff asks.

"Hillary's wedding," Louie says. "I just found out Cathy Maloney's going to be there."

"Isn't that the chick you stood up at the spring formal?" Niko says, barely able to stifle a chuckle.

"That was forever ago. I'm sure she's over it by now," Jeff said reassuringly.

"You kidding? Women remember that stuff."

"You're going to miss my big MC speech," Ashley says. "If there's even one dry eye when I'm done, I will consider the whole evening a failure."

"Wait, we all went to university with her. How do you know Hillary?" Louie asks.

"We grew up two doors down from each other. We were inseparable until she moved away right before high school."

"Well I'm not going either," Niko says. "Hillary and I had a thing back in university and I don't think she's ever gotten over me. Besides, there's only one reason I ever go to weddings."

"Oh, I can't wait to hear this," Ashley says.

Amongst the many accolades Niko likes to claim for himself, one of them is a keen observer of the human condition. When it comes to taking note of basic human behavior, he fashions himself a modern-day Jane Goodall, scrutinizing and cataloging common societal practices. He will then come up with various theories that would identify and predict future behavior. There's his old-man-in-a-hat theory which predicts that any slow and erratic driving will inevitably be at the hands of an old man wearing a hat. Then there is his six-month-backslide theory that puts forward that no breakup is complete until the couple in question resists the get-back-together urge which always comes at the six-month mark.

But here, Jeff knew exactly what theory Niko was going to pull up. "It's his low hanging fruit theory," Jeff offers.

"If there's a wedding, there's a bride. If there's a bride, there are bridesmaids and if there are bridesmaids, there is a perfect storm for getting laid. You have the underlying romantic mythology to set the mood, the excitement-induced release of endorphins, the need to be reassured that they too are sexually attractive and when you combine all that with the free flow of wine and spirits - Low. Hanging. Fruit."

Upon consideration, Ashley finds herself to be equal parts appalled and impressed. But in the end, her reaction is ultimately dismissive. "Nice theory. You'd have no luck here," Ashley says.

Niko looks a little offended. He can't tell is she's underestimating his sexual prowess or if there are disqualifying circumstances of which he's not yet aware.

"Why? Are they single?"

"Yes."

"Cute?"

"Absolutely."

"Then that sounds like a challenge."

Again, this instantaneously causes a mixed reaction within Ashely. At first blush, it sounds like Niko wants to make one of those misogynistic wagers men love so much where they place a bet on some kind of sexual conquest. And yet, even with that being the case, she can't help but let her curiosity get the best of her. There is a part of her that needs to hear more. "Wait, you want to bet on whether or not you can get lucky with a bridesmaid?"

"Unless you're not so confident anymore," Niko counters, holding eye contact the entire time. He's daring her to take this wager.

Ashley stares him down for a few seconds. "Hundred bucks."

"Make it five hundred."

"Okay but I want to write down the terms so you don't weasel out." Ashley grabs a cocktail napkin and a pen out of her purse and writes as she speaks. "Five hundred dollars if Niko takes home a member of the bridal party from Hillary's wedding."

"Hey Jeff, you gonna come watch me make an easy five bills?"

"I don't think I can."

"That sounds more like the old Jeff Dempsey. What happened to taking on bold new adventures?"

"If you ask me to jump Snake River Canyon on a motorcycle, I'll do it. But don't ask me to go to this wedding."

"You don't want to bring Katie?"

***

Yes, I've been trying to do things the old me would have been too afraid to do. And taking my new 21-year-old girlfriend to this wedding certainly fits the criteria. But I really didn't want to go and I was sure she'd understand.

"Oh my God, we should totally go!"

On the list of sentences Jeff didn't want to hear at this precise moment, that one ranks right after, 'How about I stick this red-hot poker in your ear?' and 'Can I tell you all the wonderful ways Scientology changed my life?'

Jeff and Katie are out at a pottery café where people pass off drinking over-priced lattes and mangling clay as entertainment. Jeff is carefully working away at a still unrecognizable lump of clay spinning on a pottery wheel when Katie drops that bomb on him. She is seated across from him, painting one of her finished pieces. Jeff's clay creation suddenly collapses in a messy heap. Katie tries to stifle a laugh as Jeff attempts to reshape his clay.

"I don't know if I'm ready to go to the wedding," Jeff says in an attempt to divert focus from his shoddy craftsmanship.

"That's crazy. Why wouldn't you?"

"I feel like we'd be on display." Katie looks at him quizzically so Jeff tries to explain. "You're a very beautiful young woman and I'm...not."

"Don't be so hard on yourself. In the right backless dress, any man would find you fetching," Katie deadpans.

"What we're doing is not considered age appropriate dating and I feel like people will talk about us all night. And honestly, I just couldn't imagine a more uncomfortable situation."

"Katie?" This draws the attention of both Jeff and Katie to Derek, an impossibly handsome mid-twenties Bradley Cooper type who has approached the table.

"Derek?!!" She stands up and gives him a hug. The embrace lasts a little longer than Jeff is comfortable with.

"I'm so glad I ran into you. I just got back from overseas and I was hoping we could...get together."

The way he pauses and stumbles over 'get together' tells Jeff everything he needs to know about Derek's intentions. Katie's difficulty responding suggests she correctly inferred his intent as well.

"Um...sure." Jeff looks on in disbelief. He clears his throat. "Oh, I'm sorry. This is Derek." Katie says.

Jeff shakes his hand. Before Jeff can introduce himself... "Pleasure to meet you, sir. I'm an old friend of your daughter's."

Again, Katie tries to hold in a laugh but cannot. "This isn't my Dad!"

Derek can't fight off an embarrassed grin. "I'm so sorry. But kinda relieved." He leans into Jeff. "We were a little bit more than old friends, if you know what I'm saying."

"Yeah, I think I cracked your code."

Derek now turns his attention back to Katie. "Are you doing anything Saturday night?"

Before she can answer, Jeff finds words coming out of his mouth that surprises him as much as they do Katie. "We're going to a wedding."

Katie looks at him like she's a little impressed.

"Maybe some other time then," Derek says.

Derek gives Katie a hug goodbye and goes on his way.

"Well, look on the bright side," Katie says. "No matter what happens Saturday night, it can't be more awkward than that."

***

The wedding ceremony for Hillary and Owen at First Methodist Church was lovely and would have made any upper-middle-class WASP family proud. Short, to the point, not too religious while still including the greatest hits like 1st Corinthians 13 4-8, 'Love is patient, love is kind...' It was a real crowd-pleaser.

Four hours later, upon first entering the reception hall, it was evident to Jeff that this is an event where almost no expense was spared. Beautiful flowers fill the room, decorations of lovebirds hang from the ceiling and ice sculptures could be found almost anywhere your gaze lands. But what really told Jeff this shindig cost a pretty penny isn't anything he saw, but rather was something he heard.

After more than two decades of going to weddings, Jeff learned that the easier one can identify the official colors, the cheaper the event. For example, a basic no-frills wedding would have purple and white as the official colors. One level up would be orchid and cream while one level above that would feature mauve and eggshell. So when Jeff overheard the official wedding colors are mulberry and cornsilk, he had all the information he needed.

Jeff and Katie work their way to their table and before they sit, Jeff pulls out Katie's chair for her. Already at the table are two people Jeff doesn't know, Maddie and her husband Phil, both in their mid 50's.

"Such a gentleman. And I thought chivalry was dead," Maddie says in delight.

Jeff takes Katie by the hand. She turns to Maddie. "One of the benefits of dating someone who's old...fashioned." She turns to give Jeff a little wink which Jeff misses because he is focused on the sight of Louie who approaches in his formal best.

"Lou, nice to see that you caved."

"I found out it was an open bar." Louie sits down and gestures to the empty seat beside him. "Who's supposed to be there?"

"Louie DeLulio?"

That familiar high-pitched voice sends a chill up Louie's spine. He slowly turns around and pastes on a fake smile. Standing behind him is Cathy Maloney, a cute, petite woman to whom time has been a friend.

"Cathy Maloney!"

She takes her seat beside Louie and takes hold of both his hands and she looks deep into his eyes. "I was really hoping you'd be here tonight!"

"You were?"

"I just thought we could maybe take care of some unfinished business."

"I had a feeling you might say that." Louie turns to Jeff and speaks in a hushed yet urgent tone. "You gotta help me or they're gonna find my rotting corpse washed up on shore."

Jeff acts like he hadn't heard a word Louie just said. "Can you believe some punk kid thought I was Katie's father?"

"Or we can talk about your thing," Louie says with a shrug. "Yes, I can believe it." Jeff looks crushed but Louie presses on. "It's just about the math. Were you having sex 22 years ago?"

Jeff quickly does the math in his head. One would think he would have done this calculation already although perhaps there was a part of him that was afraid to. "I guess. I was with Tracey in Grade 12."

"Then all I'm saying is it's possible. I read somewhere about this guy who was dating an older woman and after two years, he found out she was his birth mother."

"Is this supposed to make me feel better?"

"Not really. It's more for entertainment value."

Jeff gets a determined look in his eyes, leans back and looks at Cathy. "So Cathy, how long has it been since you've seen Louie? Spring Formal was it?" Louie shoots Jeff a look of horror. Jeff leans into Louie. "Now I'm entertained."

***

Ashley stands at the MC's podium going over her notes as wedding guests mingle before the reception is about to start. Niko approaches and Ashley smiles when she sees him coming.

"Where were you?" she asks. "I didn't see you at the ceremony."

"I don't go to those. Too boring. So where are these cute bridesmaids?"

Ashley points to the receiving line where the entire wedding party is welcoming guests. Niko's gaze falls on the three bridesmaids dressed in identical purple...sorry, mulberry dresses. They are aged 9, 11, and 14. Niko's face falls.

"You screwed me big time. You gotta let me go after somebody else."

Ashley pulls out the cocktail napkin and holds it up in front of his face. "I wish I could but we're bound to the written terms of the bet." She then stuffs the cocktail napkin in the front pocket of his suit coat.

"I hope you're proud of yourself," Niko says with as much righteous indignation one can muster given he made a sexual conquest bet at a friend's most sacred and joyous event. "I don't know if I'm proud. I do know I won our bet for whatever that's worth. Oh wait, I know that too - five hundred dollars!"

***

The wedding guests seated at Jeff's table are engaged in conversation while Cathy stares intensely at Louie. She leans in close to him. "Hey, did you know I just got my third-degree black belt in Karate?"

"You can only use Karate in self-defense, right?" Louie asks, desperate to be reassured he is not in immediate physical peril.

"Yeah."

Louie exhales with relief but perhaps just a tad too soon. "But when I'm drunk those rules go out the window," she adds. Cathy turns then her head for a moment and Louie grabs her wine glass and quickly gulps down its contents. He puts it back in front of her, empty.

Meanwhile, right next to the Louie and Cathy show, Jeff looks up and finds Maddie staring at him. Maddie catches herself. "I'm sorry. It's just you're such a lovely couple. You see Phil, it's like I was telling you the other day, the cutest couples look alike."

Louie's head snaps up when he hears this. Jeff looks at Maddie with more than a little skepticism. "You think we look alike? Really?"

Now Louie gives them both a once over that comes close to shattering accepted boundaries of personal space. "They do look alike."

"You have the same eyes," Maddie says.

"Yes. Very similar facial features," Louie observes as if he's Sherlock Holmes examining a new piece of evidence.

***

Niko steps out onto the outdoor balcony. He's pissed off and needs to collect himself before he goes back inside. He stands in front of the rail and looks towards the sky.

"Why do you hate me, Universe? All I needed was one drunk bridesmaid. Was that too much to ask for?"

From behind him and just off to the right he hears the unmistakable sound of someone vomiting. Niko turns around and sees Jenny, 14, the oldest of the bridesmaids, staggering on her feet, clearly drunk. Niko looks down just in time to see her puke again, this time all over his shoes. He turns his gaze skyward again.

"Okay, now you're just being a dick."

***

At the table, Jeff pours Katie a glass of wine as he looks deep into her eyes. The waiter comes over to begin serving dinner. "Excuse me, but are these meals gluten free?"

"I'm fairly certain," the waiter responds.

"Could you find out for sure? We're allergic."

The waiter nods and goes back to the kitchen as Louie perks up. "I'm sorry. Did you say we're allergic?"

"Yeah, turns out we both have a gluten allergy."

Louie smirks as Jeff shoots him a knock-it-off look and Katie taps Jeff on the arm.

"Tell them the other thing," she prods.

Jeff hesitates with clear apprehension but ultimately relents. "We both have AB negative blood types."

"Less than one percent of the population is AB negative. Pretty cool, huh?" Katie adds enthusiastically.

Louie can barely contain his glee. "That is quite a coincidence." His joy is cut short when he notices Cathy pour herself another full glass of wine. "More wine? That's...great."

Cathy is suddenly horrified. "Am I drinking too much?"

"Not at all. Don't be silly," Louie says has he subtly pulls her wine glass away from her.

"I have to be careful about that," she says as she starts to giggle. "I tend to get...amorous when I start drinking."

Upon hearing this, Louie fumbles the wine glass and spills some of the wine on Jeff and Katie. They both stand up. Maddie is quick to take charge.

"Go put some cold water on it, quick."

Jeff and Katie hurry off, leaving Katie's phone on the table.

***

Niko is cleaning off his shoes with a wet paper towel while Jenny hovers over him, still very unsteady on her feet. "Oh My God, I'm so, so sorry."

"It's okay. I should have expected it. Just when I thought this shitty night couldn't get any shittier."

"Tell me about it. I don't even want to be in this stupid wedding."

"So why are you?"

"I didn't have a choice. For some reason she wanted her nieces to be bridesmaids." Jenny watches with great fascination as Niko tries to get all the puke off his shoes. "If you ask me, I don't think he's really the one for her."

"You don't think so?"

"Hell no! Ever since I was little, all I ever heard was how she was going to be Mrs. Niko somebody-or-other on her wedding day."

Niko's head snaps around upon hearing this. "Excuse me?"

"There's some Niko guy that she's been in love with like, forever."

"Niko Stassinopoulous?"

"Yeah. How'd you know?"

Niko's grin would put the Cheshire Cat to shame. "Just lucky I guess."

***

Still seated at the table, Louie is desperately trying to avoid eye contact with Cathy when the sound of a funky ringtone startles him. He looks over and notices Katie's phone. Louie picks it up and sees the caller I.D. photo is a 40-ish-year-old woman under the name "Mom". But there's something familiar about the image, Louie has seen it before. It's like he's seen a famous actress and he's trying to place what movie or TV show she's from. And then it hits him.

"Tracey?"

Louie immediately recalls the story Jeff recounted about having the catching-up conversation with his high school ex-girlfriend Tracey when they were at the reunion. It all falls into place for him. "No way!"

Ashley is standing at the MC podium trying to get through the obligatory parts of any wedding reception. One added agenda item is a special recognition of a relative who was no longer with them to share this special day.

"One very special person in Hillary's life is her grandmother who sadly, passed away not long ago." Louie rushes up to Ashley and desperately tries to get her attention. She ignores him and continues on. "Hillary has asked if we could have a moment of silence in remembrance of her grandmother." The room falls silent as Ashley turns to Louie.

"What, Louie? What is so important that it can't wait two minutes?"

Aware of the silence that has overtaken the room, Louie mumbles very quietly. "It's Jeff and Katie. I think..."

Ashely's frustrations are beginning to surface. "I can't hear you!"

Louie tries again, only marginally louder. "Katie's mom is Jeff's old..."

"Louie, speak up, I can't hear a word you're saying."

Louie gets right up to Ashley's face which now puts him in range of the open mic on the podium. "Jeff is boning his own daughter!" The words echoed throughout the hall as the guests gasp in unison. Ashley leans into the mic.

"And this concludes our moment of silence."

CHAPTER EIGHT

After liberally applying cold water and club soda, the stains on Jeff and Katie's clothes were reduced to the point of being barely noticeable. What was clearly noticeable was the extremely weird vibe they felt when they walk into the banquet room and see that all conversation comes to a sudden halt. They can feel every pair of eyes on them as they make their way back to their table.

"What is going on?" Katie whispers to Jeff.

"Didn't I tell you! They see a beautiful young woman with a 40-year-old guy and they have to judge."

"Really? You think so?"

"Trust me. The age difference – t hat's exactly what it is. They want to judge us? Let's give them what they want." As they reach the table, Jeff sits down on the chair and pulls Katie down so she's sitting on his lap. He pulls her in close to him and gives her the deepest, most passionate kiss imaginable. Involuntarily people around them start gasping and wincing. Jeff separates from the kiss just long enough to respond to the crowd. "That's right. That's how I roll."

***

Niko comes into the room with a new spring in his step. He practically bounces all the way up to where Ashley is sitting at the head table. "I just popped by to tell you I'm going to win that bet."

"How? Did you just finish reading *Winning Bets the Roman Polanski Way?*"

"The bet was a member of the bridal party. There's one member of the bridal party who's an adult." Niko looks down the table at Hillary who is laughing and waving at one of the guests.

Ashley gives him a dismissive wave of her hand. "Oh please! You don't have a snowball's chance in hell."

"I'm going to pull off the bride heist," Niko says defiantly.

"The bride heist!?! It can't be done."

"You better hope not."

"Who do you think you are? Some kind of dashing late 60's Sean Connery who can seduce any woman he lays his eyes on?"

Niko smiles as he waves to Hillary. "Well if I am, then you know what that makes her."

"Miss Moneypenny?"

Niko puts on his best Sean Connery impression, "Pussy Galore."

***

Jeff arrives at the table with fresh drinks. He gives one to Katie who gives him an appreciative kiss when he sits down. "You take such good care of me."

Louie sees an opening he cannot resist, "Hey, who's your daddy, right?" Katie laughs. "No seriously, who is your daddy?" Louie says in a more serious tone.

Maddie jumps in to try to ease the awkwardness. "We'd love to hear about your parents."

"Well, I never knew my father. My Mom got pregnant right out of high school and she moved away and raised me by herself. She said she'd tell me about my father anytime I wanted to know but I figure if he didn't care enough to stay; I don't care enough to learn anything about him. Besides, I've never had a pressing reason to find out who he is."

"I can think of one," Louie blurts out almost involuntarily.

***

At a quiet moment in the reception, Hillary is catching a breath of fresh air by herself on the balcony.

"You're not looking for an escape route are you?"

Hillary turns around and beams when she sees Niko approach.

"Niko, I'm so glad you could come. I wasn't sure you would."

"Why? Because of our..."

"...past? Yeah. I mean it was only a weekend," she says.

"But it was a pretty amazing weekend, was it not?"

Hillary smiles but figures it best to change the subject. "So when are you going to find a girl and settle down?"

"As soon as I'm as lucky as you and I find 'the one'."

"I'm not so sure I believe in 'the one' anymore."

"Really? You never had an idea of that one person you've always dreamed of marrying? That person who made you want to carve your initials together in a tree? That's too bad. I think every bride deserves the experience of being with her dream man on her wedding night." Niko pauses and looks deep into her eyes. "Don't you?"

***

Jeff and Katie hold hands and stare adoringly in each other's eyes. A woman walks by the table and as she passes by, "You should be ashamed!"

Jeff looks up in shock and disbelief. Before he can think of a response, a man walks by and adds his commentary as he passes through. "What you're doing is disgusting!"

Now Jeff has had enough. "Okay, that's it!" He stands up and starts marching up towards the front of the room. It is clear he has a bee in his bonnet now. Louie gets up and chases after him, stopping him momentarily.

"Jeff!"

"What is it Lou?"

"I need to tell you something," Louie says cautiously.

"Louie, you're a dear friend who is genuinely concerned for my well-being so even though I am steaming mad right now, I will listen to what you have to tell me as it must be of the utmost importance."

...is exactly what I should have said. Unfortunately, what I actually said was...

"Louie, I'm not in the mood for another one of your bullshit theories. And do you know why? Because I have actual real-life problems. I have a whole wedding hall full of people who get vocally upset every time I am affectionate with my younger girlfriend. I'm sorry but whatever new crackpot conspiracy theory you found on the internet is just going to have to wait for another time. So unless there's something else you need to tell me, I have to get something off my chest."

Louie looks at him for a second while weighing his options. "Well then, don't let me stop you."

Jeff continues on his way as Cathy comes up to Louie.

"You want to get a drink at the bar?" she asks.

"I think I'm going to need one." Louie says.

Jeff marches up to the MC podium. He takes the microphone out of the holster. Ashley looks alarmed. "What are you doing?"

"Standing up for myself, that's what I'm doing," Jeff says before turning his attention to addressing the entire hall. "I don't mean to interrupt the ceremonies but there's something I have to say. I've seen your disapproving looks and I've heard your snide, holier-than-thou comments and yeah, I used to be just like you. I thought there were rules that you didn't break. Lines that were never to be crossed. But I'm not ashamed of what Katie and I are doing."

Ashley is urgently trying to get Jeff's attention but he ignores her. "And I'm glad that your world is so black-and-white that you can look at us and say this kind of relationship is…forbidden. But Katie and I have a special connection - she's my girl – and what we share is beautiful. And if 'society' doesn't agree with it, well that's just too damn bad."

Jeff marches over to Katie, pulls her close and kisses her again. Everyone cringes in horror. Jeff and Katie go back to their seat. Ashley takes the microphone.

"Okay. Moving right along, next on the agenda is..." she catches herself. Surely, this can't be right. "You've got to be kidding me. Next is the father-daughter dance."

***

Cathy and Louie share a drink at the bar. She puts her hand on his arm. "Forgive me for being forward but do you want to come up to my suite? The walls are soundproof; nobody will be able to hear the screams."

Louie knows this is either really great or really terrible. He still can't figure out her angle or where she's going with this. "Is this something I would enjoy? Or something I may live to regret?"

"Oh I promise - you will not live to regret it."

Louie sighs. "Boy, I really wish you had phrased that differently."

***

Hillary is chatting with some guests and is now standing alone watching a clearly drunk Owen whoop it up on the dance floor with his buddies and some other guests. A slow song comes on and Niko approaches Hillary and extends his hand. "My night won't be complete until I have at least one dance with the beautiful bride."

She takes his hand and they go out on the dance floor. Niko sees Owen acting up some more. He's coming across like a jackass who's at a frat-house kegger rather than his own wedding.

"He's having a good time," Niko whispers to Hillary.

"He always does," she sighs.

"Do I detect disapproval in that tone?"

"I know it's a party but it's also our wedding. He's going to pass out the moment he hits our bed. I'm not even going to make love on my wedding night."

Niko pulls away from her so he can look into her eyes. "You know. It doesn't have to be that way." She says nothing but there is also nothing in her body language that suggests she is shutting this down immediately. "I'm sure you will be a model wife, taking care of all his needs and concerns for the rest of your lives. But tonight...this is your night. Tonight you should have everything you've ever dreamed of. Not the least of which is making mad passionate love on your wedding night. Don't say anything right now. But later, you know where to find me."

She hesitates, opening her mouth to form an answer without actually saying anything.

***

Jeff and Katie sit at their table and Jeff looks like he's upset. "I shouldn't have said all that."

"I thought it was sweet."

"No, I should apologize to Hillary." With that, Jeff goes over and finds Hillary at a table just off the dance floor. As Jeff approaches her, he passes Ashley who is standing close by.

"What are you doing?" Ashley hisses.

"I want to say something to Hillary."

"Jeff, I really don't think you should."

Jeff ignores her and walks up to Hillary who's seated at the table. Ashley follows right behind him.

"Hi. I just wanted to apologize for the big scene I created before. I know that this is your big day and the last thing I wanted to do was make it about me and my issues. I still don't get it why everybody had to make a big deal out of my love life..."

Ashley cannot listen to this any longer. "Oh, for Heaven's sake! Everyone thinks Katie is your daughter."

Jeff continues his apology to Hillary. It's as if his brain is simply unable to process what he just heard. "I'm really embarrassed now. Honestly, I can't..." He stops mid-sentence. He finally takes in what he just heard. "What was that?"

"Katie's mom is Tracey, your old high school girlfriend. There's a decent chance you're dating your biological daughter."

Jeff is suddenly uneasy on his feet. He reaches out for the nearest chair to stabilize himself. "Oh God!"

"If it makes you feel any better, nobody cares that you're twice her age."

"I think I'm going to be sick!"

"Yeah, I thought it was a long shot."

CHAPTER NINE

Jeff sits on the couch in the hotel lobby with his head buried in his hands. Katie is on her cell phone a few feet away.

"You're sure about that? Okay. Yes mom, we'll talk all about it soon." Katie disconnects the call and makes her way over to him. "So, my Mom says hi."

"Oh God, what have we done?"

"Relax, we didn't do anything. You're not my father."

Jeff's head snaps up. "I'm not?"

"No. Turns out my long-lost father is her old high school drama teacher."

"She slept with Mr. Cullen?!?"

Katie punches him in the arm. "Hello!?! You slept with my mom!"

"You're not my daughter," Jeff says as if to reassure himself that his nightmare is over.

"No. Apparently, I am the daughter of the only straight high school drama teacher."

"It's not weird, right?"

"No. It's not weird."

***

Niko is standing by himself at the reception hall entrance beside the table with the guest book when he feels two hands squeeze his shoulders from behind. He turns around to see Hillary, who has a certain look in her eye.

"You have a room here tonight?" she asks.

"No."

"Then it's a good thing I got one for us. Room 1248 at 2:00 am sharp. Think you can remember that?"

"You better write it down."

Hillary grabs the pen from the guest book and then looks for something to write on. She sees a piece of a cocktail napkin peeking out of the front pocket of Niko's suit jacket. She pulls it out and is about to write when she starts reading. It takes Niko a second to realize what is written on the paper. He starts shaking his head and waving his hands frantically, "No. No. No. Wait!"

But it is too late. Hillary is horrified as she reads out loud. "Five hundred dollars if Niko takes home a member of the bridal party?!? What is it with you people? You're all sick!" She slaps him across the face and storms off.

***

Louie wakes up alone in Cathy's bed. He smiles from ear to ear. Totally buck naked, Louie gets up and heads over to the chair in the corner of the room to grab his clothes. They aren't there. Louie frantically looks around the room. He looks under the bed, in the closet, behind the nightstand. No luck.

"Why would she take my..." He stops. A light has gone on in his head. 'Of course, this was her plan all along. This is her payback. I ditched her at the spring formal and now she's going to make me leave here naked and humiliated. Oh, this was good. She must have been planning this for a long time. Everything just fell into place for her and I walked willingly into her trap.'

Louie paces around Cathy's hotel suite bedroom "Shit! Damnit! Shit." Louie stops. He looks over at her fancy dress which is slung over a chair. A sudden calm comes over him as a disturbing smile emerges on his face. "Yeah well, two can play the payback's-a-bitch game!" He grabs her dress, stuffs it in her metal garbage can and takes a lighter and lights it on fire.

***

Niko stands outside the hotel waiting for the valet. Seeing that he is not hidden away somewhere with the bride, Ashley is overcome with joy. She sidles up beside Niko.

"Hey loser, you going home?" she asks smugly.

"Getting the hell out of here, that's for sure!"

"Great, you can drive me home." Niko says nothing and continues to pout. "Don't be sour. It's just five hundred dollars. Or as I like to call it, my trip to Barbados."

From behind them, Jenny is being escorted out the front door by her mother. Jenny's mother goes from scowling to smiling when she sees Ashley.

"Ashley, you were a great MC."

"Ah, thanks. Did you guys have fun?"

"Sure, right up until the time this one decided to get into table wine." She looks at her daughter with disappointment and disdain. "Look at you. You can barely stand up and you smell like a sewer."

"Stop yelling at me!" Jenny screams.

"You just wait until we get home. And don't even ask me how that's going to happen. Your father and I have to stay to take Hillary and Owen to the airport and I'm not sending you off with some cab driver in the state you're in."

Niko overhears this and his head snaps up to attention.

When I was in college I went back to my grandmother's house and when I looked up at the wall, something amazing happened. I finally saw the pretty girl in that picture. That time and every time ever since. See that's the funny thing about perception. Once it changes, you can never look at things the same way again.

Jeff and Katie are sitting in silence on the couch in the hotel lobby.

"Again, it's not too weird, right?"

"No. It's not too weird."

Jeff stands up and pulls her up to her feet. "So we're good?"

"We're good."

Jeff leans in to kiss her but he freezes and looks at her. She has a troubled look in her eyes. The most he can muster is a kiss on her forehead.

This can mean taking a good thing and ruining it forever.

Katie can't keep up the charade one moment longer. "It's just so weird now!"

"I know."

Or it can take a hopeless situation and turn it around completely simply by looking at the same problem from a different angle.

Niko pulls out the written bet, looks at it again and smiles. He goes up to Jenny's mother. "I couldn't help but overhear your predicament. We were just about to leave anyway. We could make sure she gets home."

A still-drunk Jenny pipes up slurring her words considerably. "Hey, I like him. He's nice."

"You're sure you wouldn't mind?" Jenny's mom asks, clearly reaching out for that lifeline Niko is offering.

"Are you kidding? It would be my honor to...take home a member of the bridal party." Niko punches every word for Ashley's benefit. She suddenly gets a look of panic as she realizes what Niko is doing.

"He can't!"

"Why not?" Jenny's mom asks.

"Yes Ashley, why not?" Niko asks, barely holding back his smug grin.

"He's...been drinking."

"I haven't had a drink all night. Maybe you could take her home. Oh wait, have you been drinking?"

"Yes," she says through her gritted teeth.

"Then it's settled, Niko you can take Jenny home."

Ashley silently fumes as she realizes she's been beaten.

Or it could show us that something we once believed so fervently...

Louie, covering himself only with pillows, sneaks down the hallway and approaches the front door of Cathy's hotel suite. Something in the corner of his eye catches his attention. He stops and turns to see Cathy in the bathroom steaming his suit with a hand-held steamer.

"Your suit was bunched up and wrinkled so I thought I'd steam it for you. I hope you don't mind."

...turns out to be something else altogether.

Louie is stunned and speechless. From the bedroom, the smoke detector starts going off. Louie runs out the door.

And so, as I go forward with this bizarre new journey, I'm going to try to roll with the new perspective it brings. One day you're looking at a picture of an old woman and the next, a young girl. And that's okay. You can't hang on to the way you used to see things. Because you either deal with this new perspective in a healthy, positive way...

Jeff and Katie in a long, but non-romantic embrace. A tight neutral hug. He kisses her on the top of her head and then pulls back and looks at her.

"The next guy better be good to you."

Katie smiles, "He'll have big orthopedic shoes to fill."

***

Niko sits behind the wheel of his car while Ashley pouts in the passenger's seat. Jenny is close to passing out in the backseat. The mother leans into Niko's open window. "Thanks again. We feel so much better knowing she's in good hands."

"You can't be too careful. There are a lot of weirdoes out there."

From out of nowhere, a naked Louie jumps in front of the car and starts banging on the hood. "Let me in! Let me in!" Louie runs around to the side and tries to open the backseat door which is locked. He starts banging on the window.

"Sorry, Lou. Nobody freeballs it in my car," Niko says as he starts to drive off. Louie follows the car banging on the windows until it pulls away completely.

...or you get left behind.

Part Four

Shenanigans

Tony Sekulich

CHAPTER TEN

Three months have passed since Jeff's near-death experience at Hillary's wedding and, aside from the occasional uncomfortably long hug from an aunt at family gatherings, he hasn't had any more incestuous close calls since he broke up with Katie. For most people, this would not be noteworthy. Not having intimate relations with a blood relative is really something one pretty much takes as a given. It's not like you're going to see anything like those occupational health & safety signs that say '271 days without first-cousin groping.' But the Katie scare shook him to his core and so he claims his victories where he can.

This could also explain why he hasn't been out there on the dating scene. It's not like he's abandoned the quest to become the new Jeff Dempsey, it's just taken different forms. For a while, he began every day with 45 minutes of transcendental yoga. This led to an important moment of enlightenment. The new Jeff Dempsey, like the old one, thinks yoga is stupid and pointless. He reached similar conclusions about origami, aquafit, and calligraphy. Although in fairness, he still thinks calligraphy is cool, he just sucks at it.

The one constant through the journey so far though has been the vlogging. No matter how unsuccessful his attempts at transformative change have been, he feels at ease sharing them while sitting in front of his webcam. And perhaps even more surprising is that people seem to be listening. Jeff doesn't have a huge following but he does have a loyal one. There is the woman in Georgia who said Jeff's high school reunion moment of clarity gave her inspiration in finding a new direction in her own life. And for some reason, Jeff's comic misadventures seem to do very well in the Philippines. What Jeff is beginning to see is that regardless of where we're from or whatever cultural biases we've grown up with, deep down we can all relate to a universal human experience. And it seems the more humiliating the experience, the more relatable it is.

So as Jeff sits down and turns on the webcam, absent is any of the trepidation that once gave him pause. He follows what has now become his pre-vlog ritual of gathering himself for a moment, taking a deep breath, exhaling and launching into it.

One of my favorite things to watch on the nature channel is when chimpanzees pick nits and bugs off each other. They call this practice social grooming. I'm fascinated by how accepting these creatures are, it's like they have no personal space hang-ups. I once picked a piece of lint of a co-worker's blouse and had to explain the incident to HR. But the chimpanzees accept it because it's simply not possible to do it themselves. It occurred to me that humans do this too, it's just that our 'social grooming' occurs with personal issues and baggage. We can easily spot delusion and self-deception in others, but never in ourselves. Like those chimps in the wild, it's up to those closest in our social group to make us aware of these issues in a careful and tactful manner.

"Shenanigans!" Niko cries out, nearly spitting his orange juice across the table. It's their Sunday brunch ritual at Jeff and Niko's apartment and this spit take has left Ashley as grossed out as Louie is offended.

"Why would you say that?" Louie says, barely able to disguise his hurt feelings. "Is it really so hard to believe?"

"That a beautiful, intelligent, and successful woman at your work is throwing herself at you? – Yeah, kind of. No offense."

"How else can I possibly take it?"

"Wait, I don't understand," Ashley says. Before she can say anything else, Louie jumps in.

"We have a new consultant working out of our office and Niko doesn't believe me when I say that she is coming up to me at work and dropping serious hints that we should... you know, get together."

"No, I get why that's preposterous...no offense." Louie throws up his hands in righteous indignation as Ashley powers on. "But why would Niko use the phrase 'shenanigans'?"

"I think I can explain," Jeff chimes in.

One of the most important parts of any friendship between guys is calling each other out on their bullshit.

Jeff rattles through a few examples from his youth to underscore his point.

A 10-year-old Jeff and Niko are walking to catch the school bus with their book bags slung over their shoulder.

"The coach begged me to play pee-wee elite hockey this year but I decided to play house league because they'd be terrible without me," young Jeff declares.

"Bullshit," Niko says immediately.

Jump ahead to their high school and the boys are eating lunch in the Holy Trinity cafeteria.

Niko scans the room and a smile creeps across his face. "Do you realize I've slept with half the female teachers at this school?"

"Bullshit!"

Technically I was right. He had only slept with one-third of them. But that last time, Sister Mariana overheard me and chewed us out for using foul language in such a Holy place. She said if she ever caught us up to such shenanigans again, she'd send us to the principal's office and we'd be suspended for a week. So ever since then, just to be safe, we said shenanigans instead of bullshit. Even after we got out of school, it was our thing and we stuck with it.

"Well you can call shenanigans all you want but I'm telling you, it's true. Why would I make that up?" Louie asks. Of course, the question was meant to be rhetorical but the opening was too great for the rest of the group not to jump in.

"Delusions of grandeur," Niko says.

"Pathetic plea for attention," Ashley follows.

"Desperate cry for help," Jeff adds.

"Can we talk about someone else," Louie pleads in a desperate attempt to get the spotlight off himself. "What about Jeff here? I haven't seen him do any great new adventures lately."

"Cut him some slack," Ashley says as she holds up a white card with some indecipherable markings on it. "He's obviously been studying Chinese iconography. What does this say?"

Jeff sighs and drops his shoulders. "It says Ashley. It's written in English."

"Wow, you really do suck at calligraphy," she says in near disbelief.

"That's coming from my life coach. Imagine where my self-esteem would be if I didn't have this top-rate support team around me," Jeff says.

It's possible Jeff struck a nerve with Ashley as her tone completely changes and she shifts into full professional life coach mode.

"You want some real talk? Okay, here it is. You've been awakened to the possibility that you can do anything you want. But the burden that comes with that is deciding what it is you really want. When you thought your life was going nowhere, you never had to give this any thought."

"I've been trying new things," Jeff protests.

"You've been throwing darts at hobbies on a dartboard as a substitute for real introspection."

"Okay, so what should I do?"

"Instead of trying to find a new passion, why not reconnect with something you used to love but don't do anymore. What's the one thing the young Jeff Dempsey could do that the new one would love to do again?"

"Maintain an erection," Niko says.

"No," Jeff says instinctively. "Well...no, no..."

"Close your eyes. Think back to your adolescence, you're alone, what did you love to do?"

Both Niko and Louie practically jump out of their chairs, dying to say something but Ashley cuts them off. "As God is my witness, if the next thing out of your mouth is a euphemism for masturbation, I'm going to punch you both right in the dick."

They both freeze, then quietly return to their chairs, looking down and saying nothing. Ashley turns her attention back to Jeff. "Become young Jeff in your mind. What is your greatest passion?"

Jeff does as he's instructed, closes his eyes and begins to visualize his younger self. After no more than 10 seconds his eyes pop open like he's had some kind of epiphany.

"Basketball," he says in a simple declaration. "I miss playing basketball."

"Then you know what you have to do," Ashley says.

"Not to throw cold water on this but dude, when was the last time you picked up a basketball?" Louie asks cautiously.

"I don't know, 15, maybe 20 years." Niko and Louie exchange a look that does not go unnoticed by Jeff. "What? I still got mad skills."

"Okay, no middle-aged white guy can ever use the term 'got mad skills' to describe himself," Niko says. "Never, ever, ever, and I mean ever."

"All I'm saying is if I joined the local men's league, I could average double figures in points and rebounds," Jeff says confidently.

"Shenanigans," Niko states emphatically.

"Please, you couldn't get a double-double if you went through a Tim Horton's drive-thru," Louie says.

"I guess we'll see," Jeff says.

***

At the Cedar Room, Niko brings a fresh round of beers and places a pint in front of Louie and sits down across from him. "I thought you were supposed to be out tonight with this mystery woman that can't keep her hands off you," Niko says with just a tad too much condescension for Louie's liking.

"If you must know, I'm having drinks with her here."

Niko gestures to the empty chair beside Louie and leans in across the table. "Is she with us right now?" Niko whispers. He turns towards the empty chair. "It's really nice to meet you. Louie's told us so much about you."

"I'm meeting her here at seven, ass-clown!"

"Then why are you here so early?" Niko asks.

"I came here to use the washroom. I couldn't go at the office, the stalls in the men's room there are disgusting."

"You could always go at home," Niko says.

"Are you crazy? I'm not going to do that in my own house, I have to live there."

"You're an odd little creature, aren't you?" Niko says with a renewed fascination with the inner workings of Louie's mind. Louie ignores him and gestures with his head to the other side of the bar. "What's going on over there?"

Niko turns around to see Ashley at a table for two with a guy. He's talking and she's laughing, there's a very strong date vibe. They both stand up and start putting on their coats. It's clear the evening is coming to an end for them.

"I guess we'll find out soon," Niko says.

Ashley and her guy hug goodbye and she spots Niko and Louie watching them. She sighs and goes over to get the grilling over with.

"Hot date tonight," Louie says as she joins them at their table.

"He just left alone at 9:30 so it couldn't have been too hot," Niko offers.

"It was fine, I wasn't really feeling it," she says.

"What's his story?" Niko asks.

"He's a writer who works as a barista to pay the bills. He was nice enough, but...he didn't pass the touch test."

"You gave him a handie?" Louie asks earnestly.

Ashley just glares at him with a 'what is wrong with you' look. She turns back to Niko. "When I was in middle school, the first boy I really fell for was Darren Myles. When I would see him, my heart would actually skip a beat. One day in art class, he came up behind to ask if he could borrow a paint brush and he touched my arm. I couldn't form words. It was like you would see in a movie when the love-struck character tries to speak but all that comes out is nonsense. It was that, except in real life. And ever since then, that's how I know when I'm really into someone."

"And that's when you give them the handie?" Louie asks. Before she can respond, Louie jumps up out of his chair. "There she is."

Niko and Ashley look towards to the front doorway to see a very attractive blonde in her late 30's wave at Louie.

"Wow, she is quite attractive," Ashley says.

"You have to break up with her right now," Niko says matter-of-factly.

***

Jeff arrives at the outdoor basketball court near his apartment looking like he stepped right out of the *Hot Tub Time Machine*. Working from the ground up, he's wearing his ancient beat up Air Jordans that he wore when he played high school basketball. Those would be where the eye is immediately drawn had it not been for the Adidas short shorts that went out of basketball style in the early 1990's. The length of the shorts means all of Jeff's pasty white chicken legs are on full display. And yet, the biggest sports fashion crime just might be combining a Larry Bird Celtics jersey with his James Worthy goggles. Anyone who watched basketball in the 1980's knows this is a cardinal sin for which there is no repentance.

Jeff had hoped to have the court by himself but, to his disappointment, a 13-year-old girl is practicing left-handed layups. She tries to take it directly to the hoop but it hits the rim and bounces out.

"You should use the backboard. The backboard is your friend," Jeff offers in a friendly way.

"Do you usually approach young girls in the park or is this a special occasion?" she asks while taking a jump shot.

Jeff is stunned. He tries to stammer out an answer but cannot. No, uh, I..."

"Chill dude, I'm messing with you. You can shoot around."

Jeff cautiously approaches and squares up for a shot. His form is pretty good but as he lets it go, he lets out a scream/moan that must be what a moose sounds like when giving birth. The pain shooting through his upper body distracts him from the fact his first shot in 20 years fell two feet short of the rim.

"Been awhile?"

"Just a bit," Jeff says preparing for another shot. The girl dribbles in and stops on a dime, pivots and launches a fadeaway that's a perfect swish. Jeff is impressed. "You play on your school team?"

"My school doesn't have a team. I come here when I just want to get away from things."

"I'm Jeff."

"Keisha. You wanna play some one on one?"

"You against me? Really?"

"Unless you got a better way of playing one on one."

Jeff nods and bounces the ball to Keisha. "You can have first ball."

Keisha checks the ball as Jeff gets in a half-hearted defensive stance. He's almost two feet taller than his opponent and can't see how she'll be able to shoot over him or rebound. Keisha starts dribbling to her right and then flashes a varsity high school worthy cross-over dribble and breaks hard to her left. The move almost spins Jeff into the ground as she breaks in alone for an easy left-handed layup off the backboard. "1-0. And you're right, by the way. Turns out the backboard is my friend."

Jeff stands there slack-jawed, still unsure of what just happened. "Shit!"

**

Louie returns to the table with two drinks while his date, Sylvia freshens up in the washroom. This gives Louie just enough time to ask Niko the $64,000 question. "Why do I have to break up with her?"

"She's the mom of one of my students," Niko explains. Louie and Ashley stare at him, waiting for the rest of the explanation. Alas, there is none forthcoming.

"You want me to break up with her because her kid is in your class?"

"Yes, exactly! Thank you."

"I think you're going to have to give us more than that," Ashley says.

"I am a grade school teacher and as such, I have to carry myself with a certain decorum and professionalism. And I'm happy to do that Monday through Friday for 38 weeks out of the year. The rest of the time, I gotta be me. And I can't do that if a school parent is part of my social circle."

"Oh come on, you're making a big deal out of nothing," Ashley insists.

"Think back to your favorite teachers, how do you picture them? Respectable? Upstanding? Societal role models?" Ashley and Louie nod in general agreement. "Wrong! Teachers, when not in teacher mode, are pretty much drunken womanizers, harlots, problem gamblers, or overall degenerates. And they're able to enjoy that lifestyle because they respect the Chinese wall between their professional and personal lives. When the Chinese wall is broken, chaos ensues."

Sylvia makes her way over and Louie stands up to introduce her. "Sylvia, this is Ashley and Niko."

She greets Ashley warmly and pauses as she shakes Niko's hand. "I know you; you're my son's teacher."

Niko gives an Oscar-worthy performance. "No way! Is that true?"

"Yes. Evan Bartlett."

"Evan, of course. What a great kid. Such a pleasure."

Sylvia looks at her drink and makes a face. "Oh dear, they forgot my twist of lime. I'll be right back."

"See, it's not weird," Louie says once she's out of earshot. "You think her kid is great."

"Please! Evan's an asshole! Break up with her immediately."

***

Three nights later, Niko is surprised to hear a knock on his apartment door. He opens it to find Ashley standing in his doorway.

"I'm really sorry to just pop by but I can't find my sunglasses and I thought maybe I left them here after Sunday brunch."

Niko walks over to the kitchen counter and retrieves a pair of women's sunglasses. He holds them up. Ashley cannot hide her joy and relief. "Oh thank God, I thought I lost them for good. A few silent moments pass. "Where's Jeff tonight?"

"He just stepped in the shower. Had his first basketball game tonight," Niko says. "How about you, did you go out with barista-writer guy again?"

"Nah, I don't think he's the one." Niko can't hide the sly smile appearing on his face. "What! What is it?" Ashley asks.

"I think I know why he's not the one."

"Go ahead, let's hear it."

"I think the reason you don't feel it for barista-writer guy is due to his lack of earning potential. Deep down, you know he represents a poor candidate to provide for you and your future children."

"Nice theory, professor. But that's not the way either I or the rest of my gender operate in 2018."

"So all that matters is that he's a nice guy, who is funny and treats you well?"

Ashley senses a trap coming, but there's no backing down. "Yes."

"Great, I'll set you up. Now that I know money's not an issue for you, there are all kinds of guys you should meet."

"Okay...great."

"Who's getting set up?" Jeff emerges from his room, his hair still wet from his shower.

"How was basketball?" Ashley asks, eager to change the subject.

"It was amazing. 26 points, 14 rebounds and eight blocks. So close to a triple-double."

"Wow, really?" Niko is not intending to call Jeff a liar but the way he asks makes it obvious this is very hard for him to believe.

Yes, really. Those numbers are all the God's honest truth. So I thought I'd run them through some of the highlights.

"...knocked my opponent to the ground, grabbed the rebound for the easy put-back..."

"...drove the lane and went left hand off the glass..."

"...ran down someone on a fast break and just when they thought they had an easy layup, WHAM, I blocked it into the fourth row. Get that weak shit outta here son!"

Jeff's recap is interrupted by the second surprise knock on the door. This time Niko opens the door to find Justine, a young girl holding up Jeff's goggles. "Hey Mr. Dempsey, you forgot your goggles at the gym. They have your address written on the strap."

Jeff rushes over and snatches them out of her hand. It's like he can't send her away fast enough. As he's shoving her out the door...

"Thanks again for playing on our team tonight. We never have enough girls show up and we would have had to forfeit without you."

"Yeah, sure. No problem." Jeff is able to get her out the door and quickly closes it. He stands facing the door for a few seconds, dreading the moment he has to turn around. He finally does and sees Niko and Ashley both with their arms folded, looking at him in an accusatory manner.

Niko finally breaks the silence. "I think the word you're looking for is...busted."

CHAPTER ELEVEN

Okay, in my defense, I did start playing in the men's game. It's just that I was a little further from peak physical condition than I first thought. Turns out that not many teams want a guy who can't get up and down the floor, box out or rebound. I had made peace with the fact that I would not see any more game action for the rest of the night when Justine approached me out of the blue.

Earlier That Night:

Alone on the bench, Jeff sits hanging his head and staring at his shoes when a young voice that snaps him out of his daze.

"Excuse me, sir? Do you want to come play with us?"

Jeff looks up and sees Justine standing in front of him. "What? Me?"

"We're playing in the other gym and we only have four girls who showed up. If we don't have five players, we'll have to forfeit."

"They won't let me play with you, I'm a grown man."

"A lot of us watched you play and the other team is fine with you playing on our team."

If it means a bunch of young girls would get to play a game that night, how could I possibly say no? It was the only honorable thing to do. And if I'm being honest, it was nice to be asked to play on a team. I was certain when I explained this to Ashley and Niko, they would see there is nothing to be embarrassed about.

Back at the apartment, in the immediate aftermath of Jeff's explanations, Niko and Ashley are in mid-laughing fit. Genuine, hysterical, doubled-over, can-hardly-breathe laughing.

When Ashley can finally form words, "Let me get this straight, your big return to basketball was against 12-year-olds?"

"Some of them were 13," Jeff says. This was supposed to make it sound better but only sent them into more fits of laughter.

Wait, wait, wait," Niko says, barely able to get out the words. "Please tell me you didn't block a kid's shot and then stand over her and say, "Get that weak shit outta here, son!"

"Of course not," Jeff says emphatically.

I really did.

***

Two nights later, Ashley arrives at a quiet, out of the way jazz bar and starts scanning the place. She's looking for someone who fits the description of Steve, an old friend of Niko's whom he believes would be a great match with Ashley. She's not sure if she's here to prove a point or because she's hoping there might actually be a connection. Either way, she's going to go through with it.

"Ashley?"

Ashley spins around to see Steve, who has come in right behind her. He's tall and fairly handsome with a winning smile. Immediately, most of her apprehension disappears and she has genuine hope for the first time tonight.

"Hi, Steve. Great to meet you."

They grab a table for two in a back corner more conducive to conversation.

"I have to say, I was a little nervous heading into tonight. This is my first blind date in eons," Ashley says.

"I'm so glad you said that, me too. And to top it off, I wasn't sure if I was going to make it here in time."

"You were late getting out of work?" Ashley asks.

"No, I was held up at the soup kitchen. It was crazy in there tonight."

Hearing this, Ashley lights up. "That's so great. I really admire the fact that you volunteer your time there. It's something I always say I'm going to do but never seem to get around to."

"Oh, I don't volunteer there," Steve says without further explanation.

The wheels start turning in Ashley's head. "You're a coordinator...social worker?" she says with just a hint of desperate pleading in her voice.

"Nope!"

Before Ashley can dig any deeper, the waiter comes over to take their drink order. Steve take Ashley by the hand, "Hey, I know what you're thinking but you can relax. Order whatever you want, your drink is on me tonight."

"Drinks are on you? That's very kind."

"Drink," he says, stressing the singular.

"Of course," Ashley says, sneaking a glance at her watch.

***

The Cedar Room is for Niko what the Fortress of Solitude is for Superman. It's more than just a building, it's a fundamental part of who he is. It's where he drinks, eats, occasionally sleeps, and more than occasionally has sex. It's where he lies about falling in love. It's where he's broken up more engagements and marriages than he can count. But more important than all of that, it's a place where he doesn't have to be Work-Niko.

As he sits across from Louie and Sylvia, smiling and nodding at some story about how she had such a hard time putting Evan to bed when he was a toddler, he's not really listening to what she's saying.

His brain is currently occupied, running through a list of non-traceable poisons he'd like to slip in Louie's drink right now. Is Cyanide traceable, he thinks to himself. What about ricin? Was that what Walter White used in *Breaking Bad?*

After making a mental note to find himself a good ricin guy, he looks up to see Sylvia and Louie staring at him.

"Well?" Louie asks.

"Come again," Niko says.

"Are you able to tell in class when Evan hasn't had a good night's sleep?" Sylvia asks.

"Oh, yeah. He can be quite the drowsy little rascal," Niko says as politely as he can through gritted teeth.

"I just think it's great that we can all hang out together," Louie says.

"I never thought I'd be out with my son's teacher having drinks but this is fun," she says.

"Yes. A real delight," Niko says stone-faced.

"Oh my God! Isn't that what's-her-name?" Louie says gesturing over Niko's shoulder.

Niko turns around to take a look and then whips back around lightning quick.

"Nope, no, no. I don't believe it is."

"Yes it is. How can you forget her?" Louie turns to Sylvia. "Get this, Niko goes to her place and they start going at it right on the living room floor. They don't even make it to the bedroom when he..."

"No, no, no, no, no. I think you have me confused with someone else," Niko insists.

"What? Come on. Long story short, he's sexting her sister while he's doing it with her."

Sylvia can't hide her look of shock and horror.

"I assure you, Louie has his wires crossed," Niko says, almost pleading.

The woman in question comes over and stops at their table. "Hi, Niko."

Niko is in hell and he's wearing a wool sweater. "Hey, how are you? You remember Louie and this is Sylvia."

The woman shakes their hands. "Hi, I'm Barb. You guys having a nice time?"

"The best," Niko says. "And yourself?"

"Great, I'm just meeting up with some friends from work. I should go join them. Very nice to meet you. Great to see you again, Niko."

"You too, thanks for stopping by and saying hi," Barb starts to walk away and Niko exhales with a sigh of relief.

Suddenly Barb stops, turns around and points to Sylvia. "Oh, and try not to fuck her sister."

The following week, I went back for my second men's league game because as humiliating as the experience was, I believe that the only thing to do is get back on that horse...eventually. No one ever said you have to get on the horse right away. Maybe the horse is still in a bad mood, or it's just an asshole and maybe you should wait for another horse. The point is, instead of suiting up and playing that night, I found myself drifting into the other gym to see how the girls were doing in their game.

Jeff settles into a seat in the bleachers at one end of the gym just as warm-ups are coming to an end. They have the bare minimum of five players so Jeff is happy to remain a spectator for the game.

From her position on the court, Justine catches him out of the corner of her eye and runs over.

"Mr. Dempsey, you came. Are you going to coach us?"

Jeff is taken aback by the question. "No, no. I'm not a coach, I just wanted to see you play."

"Well, enjoy it because we're losing one of the girls and with four players and no coach, we're going to have to fold after this game."

The ref blows the whistle tosses the ball up for the opening tip-off. A smiling mom leans into Jeff. "Which one is yours?"

"None, I used to play on the team," Jeff says. This draws a look of confusion and contempt from the no-longer curious mom.

One thing I noticed about sports-parents is they're super intense and when they yell from the stands, they seem to lose all sense of double entendre. Why is it everything they yell out is begging to be followed with, "That's what she said."

"Get it up hard!"

"Watch the backdoor penetration!"

"You have to cradle the balls!"

I don't think that last one was talking about basketball. And I have to admit, even I found it difficult not shouting out from the stands.

"Justine, cheat right!" The ball goes out of bounds near Jeff and Justine comes over to inbound it. Jeff gets up and leans in for a quick word of advice. "Tell Allyson to stop dribbling into the corner. When she does, they trap her and she turns the ball over every time. Also, their point guard can't go left. She keeps selling you on the fake left and then dribbling right. She can only go right, so take that away and you'll take her completely out of the game."

"Careful there, Mr. Dempsey. You're almost starting to sound like a coach."

***

Niko stands at the front of his class in full Work-Niko mode. Wearing a navy-blue sweater over a shirt and tie and gray dress pants, he looks like he's dressed up as an insurance salesman for Halloween. Of course, for these kids, they only see this version of 'Mr. S' as he's known to them. And just as important as not bringing Work-Niko into his social sphere, he is equally as determined to keep Regular-Life Niko out of his professional environment. He takes his job seriously and would almost never let his personal life compromise his professional ethics.

Almost.

The bell sounds and the students start filing out at the end of the day.

"Evan, can you hang back for a minute," Niko says.

The nine-year-old gets teased by his friends but does as he's requested. "Sure thing, Mr. S, what's up?"

"So, I read your social studies report."

"And..."

"It was good. Very well written. Almost too well written. So I decided to put some of it through a plagiarism filter and you'll never guess what I found."

Evan starts to shift uncomfortably on his feet. "Ummmm."

"Yeah, exactly."

"Am I in big trouble?"

"Well that depends, let me ask you this. What do you think of your Mom's new boyfriend?"

Evan is completely confused now. "He's okay, I guess."

"Would you be really upset if they broke up?" Niko asks.

"I don't care. What's going on?"

"You see Evan, plagiarism is a serious offense. It would be unethical of me not to report you to the Principal for further discipline, and almost certainly a suspension. Just as it would be unethical of me to ask you to try to convince your Mom that she shouldn't see that guy anymore."

Evan starts nodding. "I'm listening."

"So the last thing in the world I would do is suggest I could let this go with a clean rewrite and no punishment if somehow you got them to break up."

Evan ponders this for a few seconds and gives Niko a nod.

***

At first glance, Ashley has reason to hope that the second Niko set-up date would go much better than the first. Kevin, late 30's, is dressed in business attire: dress shirt, tie, and black dress pants, and has a very nice smile. They have a quick coffee with no immediate red flags. In fact, when she tried to pay for her coffee, he insisted that ladies need not reach for their wallet when out on a date with 'The Kev-ster.' Referring to one's self as 'The Kev-ster' would normally be enough to send her running for the hills, but Ashley appreciated the sentiment and, after the last disaster, had adjusted the bar for what constituted a deal-breaker.

He wouldn't tell her where he was taking her to dinner so she was completely blown away when they arrived at a beautifully elegant restaurant with a private room featuring a sign that read, '*Happy Silver Anniversary Marty & Paige.*'

"Okay, I hope you don't think this is weird but I thought, what better setting to get to know one another than at a happy couple's celebration of love? There's something about being surrounded by family and friends that...I don't know, I just think is awesome," he says bashfully.

Again, a month or two ago and Ashley may very well have been weirded out by this. But there was something undeniably sweet in his approach, so she decided to go with it and give it a chance.

At a table in the back, they shared drinks and were enjoying an amazing roast beef dinner. Kevin was smart, charming, and more than held up his end of the conversation.

"Can I get you another drink?" Kevin offers in his most gentlemanly fashion.

"That would be lovely, thank you," Ashley says. With Kevin at the bar, a woman in her early 50's sits down in the seat beside Ashley.

"Hi, sweetie, are you having a good time?" she asks kindly.

"I really am. This is such a beautiful event and everything is just perfect."

"I'm so happy to hear that. Can I ask how you're connected to the family?"

"Oh, I'm not. I'm here with Kevin," Ashley explains.

The woman makes a face that indicates this does not compute. Now it's Ashley who is confused. She points to Kevin standing at the bar.

"Kevin, over there at the bar. He invited me as his date."

"There's no Kevin on the guest list," she says sternly. Ashley looks towards the bar one more time and sees a panicked Kevin flee the scene as fast as he can. Ashley is mortified and tries to explain.

"I think there's been a mis-"

"No, I know exactly who you are. You think I don't know about you and Marty?"

"Oh God!"

Now the woman stands up and starts to scream across the room.

"Is this her Marty? Is this your little whore? You brought your whore to our anniversary party? You've got some nerve!"

Ashley sinks in her chair.

**

Jeff is out for a walk trying to get his head straight. Feeling torn by two strong forces pulling him in opposite directions, he doesn't know which way to go. On the one hand, he really wants to help out Justine's team. He remembers how much playing the sport meant to him in his youth. In fact, had it not been for his complete emotional breakdown, getting together with his old team would have been the most memorable moment from his high school reunion. The girl's team needs a player and he knows of a highly-skilled middle school girl without a team.

And herein lies the problem. How does a middle-aged man track down and approach a 13-year-old girl without setting off alarm bells all across the city? And even though his intent is pure, one could even say noble, he is aware that he needs to tread carefully.

He knows her name is Keisha and she goes to a school that doesn't have a girls basketball team. He could find out what schools in the area don't have girls' teams and cross-reference those with any students named Keisha. Of course, even if he were to successfully execute this task, it would place him well into the cyber-stalker zone, a label he was barely able to shed after the Katie incident. And just hanging out outside the school, hoping to run into her is a sure-fire way to end up on a 'special list.'

Whether intentional or done subconsciously, Jeff realizes that his aimless path was taking him to the neighborhood park where he shot hoops before. Maybe there's someone that he can shoot around with. This was always his favorite way to take his mind off things when he was a kid. He would spend hours alone on an outdoor court, just shooting his troubles away. Just like Niko, Jeff had his own Fortress of Solitude.

So, as he's nearing the court, Jeff is encouraged by the familiar sound of a ball bouncing against the blacktop and then off a backboard. As he turns the corner in full view of the court, he stops and smiles. Call it fate, call it luck, or call it Deus Ex Machina, but here is Keisha shooting baskets all by herself.

"I have a proposition for you," Jeff says, immediately regretting the phrasing.

"Seriously dude, you have to turn the creep factor down like seven notches," she says, launching another shot.

"I have an opportunity for you. Do you wanna play on a team this year?"

Keisha stops and thinks about for a few seconds. "No."

"No??? Why wouldn't you want to play?"

"Because I don't generally like other girls my age. They're catty and moody and they like to team up and be mean to other girls."

"I think that's a bit of an over-generalization. I'm sure that's not always the case."

"I don't know what teenage girls were like in the 1940's, but you're in way over your head here."

"How old do you think I am?" Before she can answer, Jeff throws out another offer. "How about I play you for it?"

"Play me for what?"

"One game to 11, win-by-two, winners ball. I win, you come play for the team. You win, you never see me again."

Keisha thinks about it, smiles and bounces him the ball. "Let's do this!"

***

Niko is holding court at his usual table in the Cedar Room when Louie comes in with a spring in his step. He pulls up a chair at Niko's table.

"You look you're in a good mood today, is everything okay in your world?" Niko gently probes.

"Things are great now. It was touch-and-go for a while, but everything is cool now."

"What do you mean touch-and-go?"

"It was the weirdest thing, all of sudden the kid starts making this fuss like she's spending too much time with me and he doesn't like the fact that we're dating. He was being a real prick about it."

"And that didn't cause her to end it with you?"

"It almost did. But I figured I'd just buy him off. Cost me a new iPhone and a semi-automatic paintball gun but after that, we were best friends again."

"That's just great."

Niko would have pressed further but a voice coming from behind him brings the other conversation to a screeching halt. "What. The. Fucking. Fuck!?!"

Niko doesn't have to turn around to see who it is or inquire what it's about. "How was your date with Kevin?"

Ashley sits down across from him, lasers shooting from her eyes. "You mean 'The Kev-ster?' It was fantastic. I can't decide if my favorite part was unknowingly crashing a 25th Anniversary dinner, being publicly accused of being the guest of honor's 'little whore' or watching my date flee the scene when it all went down."

"Yeah, he does that," Niko says casually. "He's a free-foodie. He prides himself on finding the best free meals in town. Great guy though."

"I know what you're trying to do. You're setting me up with these broke-ass losers trying to prove a point. But you're not going to define me with your little games."

"You want a real candidate, great career, well-off, likes to spoil his dates? Ok, let me do one last one. I promise this guy is not a broke-ass loser."

Ashley stews but doesn't respond. Then finally, "I'll think about it."

Louie sees Sylvia arrive at the bar and goes to greet her. Ashley makes a face as she sees them laugh and kiss.

"How are they still together?"

"I'm asking myself that very same question."

"Well, what can you do?" Ashley asks rhetorically.

"I've given some thought to that," Niko says. "And I was really hoping it wouldn't come this but, it looks like he's left me no choice."

"What are you talking about?"

"The nuclear option," Niko says solemnly.

CHAPTER TWELVE

I'm sure nobody will be shocked to discover that I handily defeated Keisha in our one-on-one matchup 18-16. It was never really close. And this presented a good news-bad news scenario for me. The good news is, by winning, I kept the team together and am now solely responsible for leading a group of 13-year old girls. The bad news is, by winning, I kept the team together and am now solely responsible for leading a group of 13-year-old girls. Look, they're great kids and I get the sense that they really do want to learn and get better. It's just that Keisha may not have been completely off the mark about their attitudes. It's like they sometimes have a hard time keeping off-the-court issues from showing up on the court.

Jeff paces the sideline during the team's fourth game since he brought in Keisha to join the team. They managed to win two of the three and with a win today, will qualify for a huge regional tournament this coming weekend. And from where they were when Jeff was one of their players, earning that spot will feel like an NCAA March Madness Tournament bid.

On the court, Maddie sees a wide-open Keisha under the basket, but rather than passing it to her, takes a tough contested shot that barely grazes the rim and bounces out of bounds.

"Maddie, no! She was wide open!" Jeff turns around, muttering to himself. "Why will she not pass the ball?"

"Coach," Justine's attempt to get Jeff's attention from the bench draws a quick harsh glare from him. "Sorry....Jeff."

Jeff does not want to be called coach. He feels being called coach would make it seem like he's taken on the job permanently and that is something he has outright refused. He's just holding down the fort until their real coach arrives. By being called Jeff, it keeps that non-committal aspect at the forefront.

"Yes, Justine?"

"You know why Maddie never passes to Keisha, right?"

"I have no idea."

"One day after practice, a bunch of us went to the mall and Dylan was there. He's a guy that she's majorly crushing on. We're all shipping them huge. Anyway, later on, Maddie saw Keisha being all friendly with Dylan and that was it for her."

Jeff processes this for a few seconds before coming to a horrifying realization. "My point guard won't pass to our best forward because she saw her talking to a boy in the mall?"

"Pretty much."

Jeff spins around, looking for the referee. *"TIMEOUT!"*

The girls gather round.

"Maddie, five times you had Keisha wide open and didn't make the pass. When you see an open teammate under the basket, I don't care if she stole your favorite Backstreet Boys CD, pass her the damn ball."

"What are Backstreet Boys?"

"What's a CD?"

Jeff is incredulous. "Maddie, are you hearing me? Pass the ball!"

"Oh. My. God. If you tell me to pass the ball one more time, I'm literally going to kill myself," Maddie says with full drama-queen flare.

"That might be a bit of an over-reaction," Jeff says.

"Well duh, Einstein. I wasn't really going to do it. I was being ironic."

"No, you were being hyperbolic. It's ironic that you don't know the difference."

Wow. Where did that come from? Clearly, I'm spending too much time around Niko.

***

Only after Niko swore on his ability to get an erection that Richard had no money issues or miserly tendencies did Ashley agree to go on yet another setup. But after her previous two experiences, she is going to exercise extreme caution. At first, everything about Richard seems perfectly fine. In his mid to late 40's, Richard has a distinguished attractiveness to him. He is impeccably dressed and is incredibly charming. When he picks the perfect red wine to go with her New York strip steak, Ashley is beginning to regain actual hope. But that's exactly when everything fell apart for her before, she reminds herself.

Still, the night progressed without even the tiniest hiccup. Through their dinner, Ashley learned the following:

Richard is divorced with two teenage children in high school.
He works on Bay Street as a financial analyst.
He likes to spend time in the summer on the open water on his 25-foot sailboat.
He loves animals but prefers dogs over cats.
He does a wicked Karaoke performance of Come on Eileen including all of the Gaelic parts.

When he suggests that they go for after dinner drinks to a small club around the corner, Ashley is only too happy to say yes. At the club, they are shown to a cozy table next to the fireplace near the back. She orders a red wine, he orders a scotch and he takes her by the hand.

"I don't want to get way ahead of myself but I really feel this connection with you."

"I think you're pretty great," Ashley says, careful not to get too far ahead of herself.

"I just feel like I don't have to pretend around you. You know, the usual first date bullshit where you try to present this version of yourself that's not real."

"Yeah, I know what you mean," she says.

He stares into her eyes then leans in closer. "How about a widdle kissy-wissy?"

Ashley couldn't decide what was more alarming – that he asked for a kiss or the way he did it. Don't freak out, she tells herself. It's not a big deal. She leans in and gives him a quick peck.

About 30 minutes later, he looks at his watch and yawns. "So late. Wittle-Wichie needs to go beddy-bye."

Ok, what's happening here, Ashley asks herself. Does this guy have some kind of weird baby fetish or is this just his way of trying to get me into bed? Within 15 seconds she would have her answer.

"Uh-Oh! Baby made a boom-boom in his diaper."

"That's it, I'm done!" she says as she stands up and marches straight out of the bar.

***

Late in the second half, Jeff's team trails by one as he stands on the sidelines during a time-out. He scribbles frantically on his clipboard as his team looks on.

"Okay Keisha, you're here," he says, marking an 'X' on the clipboard. "Now show me where Dylan was when he came up to you in the mall." She rolls her eyes and points to a spot on the clipboard to her right. "Right, so he comes in like this and starts talking to you, you didn't initiate the conversation."

"I told her that already. I don't even like him."

"Ok, here's the game plan. Keisha you're going to send him a text telling him that you don't like him in that way. Now Justine, here's where you come in, you're going to strike up a conversation with Dylan at school and suggest he should give Maddie a call."

The girls react like he just suggested she should chew off her own arm at the elbow – equal parts horror and disgust. "Only your parents call you on your phone," Maddie says. "Be like a normal person and Snapchat."

"Ok then," Jeff says as patiently as he can. "Tell Dylan to send Maddie a snap...chat. I guess. Is that cool with everyone, are we good?"

The team nods reluctantly.

"Okay then, if there are no more beefs to squash, can we please go qualify for the tournament?"

***

No neighborhood is 100 percent safe but Jeff and Niko's apartment is located in a part of the city where the most common criminal activity is the illegal downloading of *Downton Abbey*. Because of this, Niko has never gotten into the habit of locking the door behind him when he comes home. This is such a non-issue, it's not something he's actually given any thought to.

Until now.

Sitting on his living room sofa, about to take his first bite of Shanghai Noodles from his favorite Hakka-Chinese place around the corner, his apartment door flies open and Ashley storms in.

"Thanks for THAT!"

"Please, come in."

"What is wrong with you?" Ashley says as both a question and a statement.

"Things with Richard didn't work out? The baby thing didn't do it for you?"

"No, I think the deal-breaker was when he shit his pants and wanted me to change him. Why can't I find a decent, normal guy?"

"Still nobody who can pass the touch test?"

"Not with that parade of losers you've been sending my way. I know this sounds petty but what does it say about me that Louie is in a relationship and I'm not?"

"Oh, I wouldn't worry about that. That's over and done with," Niko says matter-of-factly.

"Really, what happened?"

"It may or may not have been something I did."

"Wait, was this the nuclear option?"

Niko gives a little wink.

Two Days Earlier...

Niko and Louie are having a beer at the Cedar Room.

"Hey Lou, did you ever resolve that filthy washroom issue at your work?"

"No. I send them emails but they say it's up to the building management and they aren't doing anything about it."

"That's not right," Niko says. "You have a right to sanitary conditions at your workplace. Somebody needs to do something!"

"Well yeah, but what can you do?"

Niko appears to be thinking it over. Miraculously, he is struck by a brilliant idea. You know what you could do, just as an easy temporary solution. You could get your company to put disposable paper toilet-seat covers in all the washrooms."

Louie ponders this and begins to nod.

"I mean, it's not a permanent solution," Niko continues. "But it's an easy fix that would provide you guys some immediate peace of mind. They would only need them for the men's rooms because the ladies' rooms are always clean, that's obvious to everyone."

"Yeah, that would be better," Louie says. "I'm going to ask them to do that."

"No, you're going to <u>demand</u> they do that. And the key is to do it when everyone is around so there are witnesses when they have to say yes."

Louie is getting excited about this. "Yes, yes. I will not take no for answer."

"But you need to make sure that they don't cheap out and get any no-name toilet-seat covers. You gotta get the very best."

"What's that?" Louie asks.

"Well, you know how you don't want just any facial tissue, you want Kleenex. And you wouldn't settle for any flying disc, you want a Frisbee. In the same way, you can't settle for any brand of toilet seat cover..."

The Following Day

"I'm sorry, could you say that again? There's no way I heard you right."

To say Louie's boss was baffled would be a bit of an understatement. Louie has always been as much of an odd duck at work as he is around his friends. But even for him, what his boss thought he just heard was beyond bizarre. Especially in a conference room filled with key players on their big project, one of them being Louie's new girlfriend, Sylvia.

"Oh, you heard me just fine. I have to insist that the company install Glory Holes in all of the office washrooms," he says proudly. He's met with blank stares and looks of horror. "Well, not all of them, just the men's rooms for reasons which should be obvious to everyone."

"Louie. I don't think this is an appropriate suggestion for a workplace," his boss says in a soothing manner, attempting to get Louie to back off this idea before he causes any more embarrassment.

"Look, I know it seems weird at first. God knows they're not something I ever thought I'd want to use, but I tried one last night and...wow, what a feeling! To be honest, I don't think I can walk into a men's room now that doesn't have Glory Holes."

"Louie, I think you should drop this."

"No, I am not going to drop this. I work hard for this company. I give it everything I've got and I don't think it's asking too much for when we need those five minutes of private time, an employee can walk into a men's room and enjoy the blissful sensation that only a Glory Hole can provide. You don't believe me? You try it just once and I promise you, we will be Glory Hole buddies for life!"

***

Ashley struggles to catch her breath. "Why would he possibly believe there are toilet seat covers called Glory Holes?"

"I may have shown him a dummy website with packaging and photos of the product," Niko explains. "And it's possible I had a sample made up for him to try."

"How long did that take you?"

"The photoshopping and website design hardly took any time at all. But do you have any idea how hard it is to get a glory hole domain name that's not already taken? I guess people must really love their toilet seat covers."

"How do you know they broke up over it?"

"Evan came up to me before class today to tell me his mom broke up with her boyfriend. And she can never, ever, ever tell him why," he said with a trace of a proud smile.

Jeff walks through the door and hangs up his coat.

"How did the game go?" Niko asks.

"Once I got Bette Davis and Joan Crawford to pass to each other, great. We qualified for the tournament Saturday."

"That's awesome, congratulations," Ashley says.

"They're actually starting to gel into an actual team. Our game is at 3:00 pm if you want to check it out."

"You what, I just might do that," Ashley says.

***

The early stages of Jeff's first tournament game as pseudo-coach are going as well as he could have hoped. The girls are playing as a team – determined and focused. In fact, the only one not 100% focused on the game is Jeff himself. Throughout the game, he's been casting glances back towards the stands. He is doing this so frequently that the girls on the bench nudge each other and gesture toward him whenever one catches him doing it.

"Coach...? Jeff!" Keisha exclaims, finally snapping Jeff's attention back to the game. "They called timeout. What do you want us to run here?"

"Right." Jeff grabs his clipboard and starts to diagram an inbound play.

"You expecting someone?"

"No, why would you ask that?"

"Some woman seems to be waving at you from the stands," Keisha smirks.

Jeff looks around and sees that Ashley has made it to the game. He smiles, waving back at her before turning his attention back to his sort-of-coaching. This draws a collection of Ooooohhhh's from the girls.

"Ladies, ladies, calm yourselves. That's Ashley, she's just a friend."

"You sure about that?" Keisha asks.

"Yes," Jeff responds confidently.

"Good thing then, because it looks like her smokin' hottie boyfriend just showed up."

This causes Jeff to whip around so fast that he bumbles and drops his clipboard. Frantically scanning the crowd, he sees that the smoking hottie boyfriend is actually Niko, who was late coming in. Jeff exhales deeply.

"That's not her boyfriend, that's my roommate."

I sometimes wonder if those chimpanzees would be better or worse off if they could groom themselves. Yes, they could do it anytime they needed without relying on a partner but...maybe they'd lose something by not having that social bonding. I mean, it would be great if we could see our own shenanigans and address it ourselves but the fact is, we're often too close to it to see it objectively. We need an outside perspective to do our emotional social grooming for us. Whether it's to stop fighting a label that so clearly applies...

The team goes back onto the court but Keisha hangs back and leans into Jeff. "Yeah, she's just a friend like you're not really our coach. Take a look. You got me to join the team, you got Allyson to stop dribbling into the corners and you got that hateful witch to pass me the ball. I hate to be the one to break it to you but..."

Curious as to the cause of the delay, the referee sprints over to the bench. "Hey, Coach!"

"Yeah, that's me," Jeff says without immediately realizing the implication of what he just said.

Of course, there can be times when people misinterpret where we're coming from and draw unfair conclusions from a simple utterance...

Realizing what he just said, Jeff involuntarily blurts out, "Son of a bitch!"

Unfortunately, the referee, convinced that Jeff was talking to him, tosses Jeff from the game.

Or perhaps from a well-intended but grossly misinterpreted speech.

Louie walks down a long hallway eventually coming to a door that reads 'Sexual Addiction Counselling.'

But more often than not, the perspective of those closest to us is the only way we can see what we need to. To break through the lies, facades, and self-delusions we create to protect us from truths we aren't ready to face.

Relegated to watch the rest of the game as a spectator, Jeff takes an empty seat in the stands behind Ashley and Niko.

"What just happened?" Niko asks.

"I have no idea," Jeff says. He leans in close to Niko and Ashley so they can hear him. "Look, I really wanted to thank you guys for showing up today." To help steady himself, he places his hands on Ashley's shoulders. "It really means a lot to me."

Ashley tries to speak but suddenly finds herself unable to form a sentence "Uh... yea...sure...I..uh."

"Whoa, what's happened here? Looks like we lost radio contact with this one," Jeff says.

But one way or another, those facades will crumble when we least want them to. And it can show us that maybe the reason you were set up on a series of loser dates was not to prove that you are shallow and materialistic, but that you can't recognize a prince until somebody shows you a bunch of frogs.

Ashley is mortified that this moment of awakening happened in front of Niko who knows exactly what her reaction meant. When she finally looks over and makes eye contact, he doesn't react with surprise. Instead, he just gives her a knowing wink.

And if you're lucky, this sudden revelation, horrifying as it may be, will be exactly what you need.

Tony Sekulich

Part Five

UP IN HONEY HARBOUR

Tony Sekulich

CHAPTER THIRTEEN

When I was 14, I worked up the nerve to ask Cynthia Randall to go to the movies. When she said yes, I looked for the most romantic movie I could find in theaters in the late summer of 1990. Given a choice between Flatliners, Presumed Innocent, and Ghost, I figured the safest bet was the one with the guy from Dirty Dancing.

Turns out it was the right choice. The movie was an instant classic and, until millennials hijacked the term, 'ghosting' someone meant appearing shirtless behind them and ruining their pottery. I know it doesn't sound like much but you really have to see the movie to appreciate the romance.

The only problem was that Cynthia's annoying little sister wanted to tag along and Cynthia didn't know how to get rid of her. I told little sis that Ghost was one of the Poltergeist movies and she wouldn't be allowed in the theater.

The only reason I was able to scare off the sister was because ghosts can take many forms and mean different things to different people. They can be cute and funny like in Casper or Ghostbusters; romantic like in Always or Ghost; or terrifying like in Poltergeist or The Haunting.

I think it's like that with life's figurative ghosts as well. Sometimes we come face to face with choices we made in our past and they either validate us or haunt us. There are friendly ghosts that confirm that we made the right choice way back when, or terrifying apparitions that make us wonder where everything went so wrong. The problem is, when we're making these critical choices, we have no idea which way it will go. Every decision feels like the right one when we make it. And we won't know which way it will go, until one day...when we do.

"Casual? Open-toe? Dressy? Semi-dressy? What do you think?"

Ashley's request for advice on the appropriate footwear to pack was fairly straightforward and could have been easily answered in moments. Of course, you would never know that from the blank stares she's currently receiving from Jeff, Niko, and Louie who are gathered at the Cedar Room for a cool refreshing beverage. The silence is broken by Niko who punctuates the moment with his patented Niko candor.

"I don't give a shit, bring whatever you want," he says.

"Not to be the stereotypical female, but packing for a getaway weekend is more involved for me than it is for you. You're guys. You could show up anywhere in overalls and sandals and get away with it. I need to know, am I going to any events while I'm there? Am I going to a restaurant? Is it a super-classy place or could I get away with semi-dressed-up? Will there be a function where I need to dress garden-party chic?"

"I'd say it's more like upscale gentlemen's club chic," Niko says.

"In this little fantasy of yours, am I the stripper or am I getting the lap dance?" Before anyone can answer, "You know what, never mind."

"No, no, no," Louie jumps in. "Please go on, spare no detail."

As that moment of awkwardness hangs in the air, Jeff attempts to get the conversation back on track. "Where are you going for your little excursion?"

Now all three of them stare at Jeff with confused looks.

"You didn't tell him?" Ashley asks Niko directly.

Niko is searching for a way to answer when Louie bails him out. "Niko invited Ashley to the cottage for Canada Day."

"The boys weekend?" Jeff says, oblivious to the implied protest in the question.

There are few things more sacred amongst a group of guys than an annual cottage weekend in the summer. Sometimes the only thing that will get you through another frigid northern winter is the thought of getting drunk and having a speedboat pull you around a lake on an inner tube.

Some of the more popular Canadian summer celebrations include May 2-4 weekend, Canada Day, and Bonhomme's Birthday. For Jeff, Niko, and Louie, their annual summer getaway is spending the Canada Day weekend at the cottage. Canada Day is the national holiday celebrated on July 1st and no matter what day of the week it falls, Canadians make a long weekend out of it. When it falls on a Wednesday, the country essentially comes to a standstill for the entire week.

Nobody questions it and most Canadians simply accept it as a birthright. No different from universal healthcare, global hockey domination, and feeling smugly superior to Americans.

Like a majority of the population of Southern Ontario, for Canada Day the boys make the trek about three hours north of Toronto to a region known as 'cottage country.' Their specific destination is Niko's family cottage in Honey Harbour on Georgian Bay.

When Niko's parents moved out west in his early 20's, taking care of the cottage fell on him alone. Being a teacher, the situation is ideal. From the time school lets out in June through Labour Day, Niko spends the summer up in Honey Harbour. And the summer doesn't officially start until Jeff, Louie and some others come up for what has now become the most important three days of the year.

It's not that Jeff is opposed to Ashley joining, he was just thrown by the idea of a woman joining the group. Most of the women who end up at the cottage are there by way of special invitation by Niko. That 'special invitation' is usually a picture of his junk with the caption 'You like?'

Or at least that's what Jeff is telling himself. The real reason Ashley's invitation has Jeff discombobulated is that he still hasn't sorted out his feelings towards her after his pseudo-awakening at the basketball tournament. The girls on the team were right. He did have a flash of jealousy when he thought Ashley had brought a new guy to the tournament.

But what does that mean? He doesn't really think of Ashley in that way. She's been an amazing friend and she's really helped him feel better about his life ever since the night of the high school reunion. He hasn't completed the journey of becoming the new Jeff Dempsey, but he's also no longer overwhelmed by the sense of hopelessness that once consumed him. Even that progress would not have been remotely possible without her.

So was that moment of jealousy a reflexive reaction to the thought of losing his guide and life coach, or is there something more? Until he has that answer, it's unlikely Jeff is going to feel comfortable in his own skin around her.

"You don't mind if I join you, do you?" Ashley asks tentatively.

"No, of course not," Jeff spits out. "That will be great. Who's up for another round? I'm buying."

"Grab me one while I hit the head. I gotta piss like nine large dogs," Louie proudly declares.

Jeff and Louie head in opposite directions, leaving Niko and Ashley alone at the table.

"You need to tell him this weekend," Niko blurts out.

"I don't think the cottage weekend is the time to bring it up."

"Are you on crack? The cottage weekend is the ideal time to bring it up. A walk on the lakeshore while the moonlight reflects off the water. You two won't be able to keep it in your pants."

"You almost composed a beautiful romantic thought there."

"I have hidden levels," Niko says.

The two sit in silence as Ashley ponders her options. "About the packing..."

"At no time will you be required to dress garden-party chic."

***

The cottage weekend routine has been well established over the past two decades and it is adhered to with the same reverence of tradition as the Vatican selecting a new Pope. The gang travels up in one car where Jeff drives and Louie is banned from picking the music. They used to rotate responsibility for selecting the tunes but that went out the window, as Louie himself nearly did, after what became known as the Macarena incident of 1996.

When they reach the town of Honey Harbour, there are two main stops for supplies. Honey Harbour Town Centre is where they pick up food, hardware, and fireworks. Just down the road is the liquor store. With four people this year, they decide to pair up. Niko and Louie get dropped off at Town Centre while Jeff and Ashley go ahead for the booze run. They will then swing back and grab the guys at the Town Centre, at which point they are no more than 10 minutes away from Niko's cottage.

Jeff and Ashley hit the booze store like a well-trained black ops Special Forces unit. In less than three minutes they are in and out with a variety of hard liquor, two mini-kegs of beer, and in a new wrinkle, a box of red wine. In fact, the only hitch in the mission comes when Ashley broaches the topic of local women with Jeff.

"I don't really know any of the locals," Jeff says to her query. "Really, I've never ventured too far away from Niko's cottage."

"Who knows, maybe you'll meet someone this weekend," she says.

Jeff processes this for a few seconds, unsure why she's saying this.

"Is that something you think I should do? You know, as my life coach."

"Do you feel like you're in a place where you're ready to get back into a steady relationship?"

Jeff is given a bit of a reprieve when the short drive to the Town Centre is over and they get out of the car to go in the grocery store looking for Niko and Louie. They walk in silence for what feels like an uncomfortable period of time.

"I think I am." Jeff finally says. "If the right situation presented itself, I can see myself with somebody."

"How will you know it's the right situation?"

"I guess it's just one of those..." Jeff is halted both in mid-sentence and in his tracks. "Holy shit!"

Ashley looks ahead to see what could have spooked Jeff but as she follows his line of sight, all she sees is Niko and Louie talking to a blond woman in her mid to late 30's. "What is it? What do you see?"

"Trouble," Jeff says solemnly.

Summer 2000

In the summer of 2000, while the rest of the Western world was being introduced to Jeff Probst and the phrase 'the tribe has spoken,' 23-year-old Niko Stassinopoulos was blissfully unaware of the birth of reality TV. Fresh off his first year as a teacher in the public school system, Niko was enjoying his first work-free summer since the tenth grade.

In homage to his favorite *Seinfeld* episode, it was known as the Summer of Niko. While Jeff and Louie were back in Toronto working day in and day out, Niko was taking advantage of all the R&R opportunities of Honey Harbour.

Mornings were usually spent explaining to the previous night's guest that he was so busy and it was a shame she couldn't stick around. This was usually followed by a boat ride with an hour of fishing thrown in for good measure. If the catch was good, he would clean it and throw it on the BBQ and wash it down with a cold Dos Equis.

In the afternoon, you could find him listening to music while working on his already perfect tan. At night, he'd head into town and chat up one of the many lovely young women visiting the area. Then he would repeat the process the next day.

On the weekends, Jeff and Louie would join him for beer, tunes, water-skiing and overall fun in the sun. It was cottage Nirvana. It couldn't possibly get better.

Until it did.

July 19, 2000

Niko and Louie enjoy a mid-afternoon beer on a patio overlooking the water. There aren't a lot of pubs in Honey Harbour but the view from this one is hard to top.

"I'm telling you, there's something to it," Louie says definitively. "These things don't get made up out of thin air."

"It's local legend, Lou. If it were real, we would have hard evidence."

"No, here's how I know it's not just made up..." Louie went on to list why his latest local myth & lore theory was real, but Niko doesn't hear any of it. His attention is diverted by a vision of loveliness entering his peripheral vision. She is slightly tall, very fit, and had her long blonde hair is pulled up in a ponytail. By Niko's best guess she is early 20's, maybe one or two years younger than he.

When he tunes back in to Louie's pontificating, he is only able to catch the tail end "...so, what do you think?"

"Maybe you are on to something," Niko says, hoping that would put an end to the conversation. He should have known better.

Louie drones on, but not long after the young blonde sits down, she is approached by a townie well into a serious day bender. Niko can only pick up bits and pieces but the drunken tool keeps saying things like "You should smile, beautiful" and "We could be real friendly to each other, would you like that?"

Niko reasoned that this could not have been the first time she had to deflect the unwanted advances of a drunken idiot. What's more, she is handling herself just fine. Niko realizes she doesn't need rescuing. On the other hand, the idiot isn't taking a hint. After coming to the conclusion that he couldn't possibly listen to Louie for one more minute, Niko knows what he has to do.

"I think you and I should take a boat ride together. How does that sound?" the drunken tool slurred.

"That's really kind of you but I don't..." She doesn't get a chance to finish that sentence. From out of nowhere she feels two hands on her shoulders. When she spins around to see who it is, Niko leaned in and kissed her on the cheek.

"Hi sweetie, sorry I'm late. Staining the deck took longer than I thought." Niko smiles and sits down, pulling his chair close to her.

Caught between two strangers, she is beginning to feel like she is living an episode of the Twilight Zone. She quickly does a threat assessment in her head and decides Niko is the safer of the two options and decides to play along.

"I told you it would," she says in a playful I-told-you-so manner.

"Oh, and your Mom said dinner Friday is a go but don't forget to order the invitations for your sister's shower. They really should have gone out weeks ago – her words, not mine." Niko turns to the drunken tool. "Is this a friend of yours? Hi, I'm Niko." Niko holds out his hand and buddy reluctantly shakes it.

"You guys have a good one," he says as he stands up and quickly exits.

Niko's somehow yet-to-be-named real-life fantasy woman stares him down with a few seconds of cold silence, before asking, "What's the deal? You get off on the whole 'knight in shining armor' shtick?"

"First of all, that is a great use of Yiddish. And no, it's not chivalry, it's sheer opportunism. I saw an opening to break the ice with a beautiful woman and voila – here we are."

"Is your name really Niko?"

"Niko Stassinopoulos. I have a cottage just a few minutes from here."

"I'm Beth. I'm spending the summer at my parent's cottage across from Jack's Rock."

"You go to university near here?" Niko asks.

"I just graduated, actually. I'm taking this summer to figure out what I should do in the fall."

"Well, hello Beth," Niko says, extending his hand. "It is a genuine pleasure to meet you."

As Beth takes his hand and holds it for just a few seconds, Niko feels a jolt of energy go through him that he had never experienced before. He always told the boys to never fall for cottage girls because what you're experiencing is nothing more than a mirage. Away from the sun and the lake and the beach, it will never be the same. But as each second ticks away and he finds himself unwilling to let go of her hand, he fears for what is about to happen.

That fear was not unfounded.

For the next few weeks, Niko and Beth are rarely apart. Beth loves to spend sunny days with him out on the boat as they tour the thousands of tiny islands nearby. At night they would watch the sunset over the lake and when it cooled off; they would go inside and warm each other up.

One afternoon, they had arranged to meet in town to grab an ice cream before heading back out on the water. Beth arrived there first and Niko sees her from afar. He starts towards her when something gives him pause.

An older man approaches Beth, giving her a warm hug and kissing her on the cheek. Niko's curiosity is too much for him to turn away. As he gets closer, he sees that the man's face is very familiar. He knows him from somewhere but can't quite place it.

When Beth sees she is in the presence of both men, she becomes visibly uncomfortable.

"Oh hi," she says as Niko joins them. "Niko, this is my father. Dad, this is Niko."

Her father! Of course, that makes sense. Niko feels all the anxiety lift away from his body...momentarily.

"Charles Secord, nice to meet you," he says, offering Niko a firm handshake. Niko gives him his best 'meet-the-dad' firm grip with eye contact and that's when it hits him.

"Superintendent Secord?" Niko says in a tone that was begging for a correction.

"One and the same." He turns to his daughter as a thought strikes him. "Be sure to get those campus housing forms in to the U of W. Freshman housing is very competitive and if you wait too long, you might not get a spot."

And that's when the second shoe drops. There are a few more minutes of conversation but Niko doesn't catch any of it. His head is ringing from the kind of anxiety that early man must have experienced after finding themselves cornered by a saber-tooth tiger.

Later, Niko and Beth find themselves alone walking towards the shoreline.

"Your dad is Superintendent Secord?"

"Yeah."

"Yeah???"

"What's the big deal?"

"I'm a teacher in his school system."

"Teachers are allowed to have personal lives."

"So do you want to tell me why you're applying to <u>freshman</u> housing?"

"It's not a big deal, I turned 18 in May."

"I'm nailing my boss' 18-year-old daughter and you can't see why it's a big deal?"

Beth shrugs and continues walking. Niko rushes after her.

"You told me you just graduated from university," Niko presses.

"No. You asked if I went to university and I said I just graduated. You assumed I meant from university."

"That's dishonest," he says.

"Not dishonesty, sheer opportunism. I saw a window to start dating a hot cottage guy and voila – here we are."

**

"Jeff!" Beth exclaims as Jeff and Ashley join the conversation. She gives him a big hug and holds both hands for a moment. "God, you guys look exactly the same. It's so great to see you all."

"Beth, this is our friend Ashley. Ashley, this is Beth." The two exchange pleasantries.

"What are you doing in these parts? I haven't seen you around here in years!" Niko asks.

"I'm just spending some time at my parent's cottage. It's their 40th wedding anniversary this year so we're having a huge family celebration."

"That sounds like a lot of fun for you," Jeff says politely.

"How about you guys? How long are you here?"

"Niko's here all summer, the rest of us are just here for the long weekend," Jeff says.

"I have to run but I'd love to see you guys and catch up," Beth says. "We're having a pre-Canada Day bash at my folks' place tonight. Mom's having it catered and we've got fireworks planned for midnight. Why don't you guys come? It'll be fun!"

"Thanks, but I don't think we can ma-"

"We'll be there!" Ashley declares.

The three guys shoot her a look with Niko's being significantly harsher than the others.

"That's great," Beth says. "Niko knows how to get there, so show up anytime after eight." She starts to walk away but then stops and turns around. "Oh, one more thing. It's a semi-dressy thing so you'll want to dress garden-party chic."

Niko cannot bring himself to make eye contact with Ashley whom he knows is giving him a look at that precise moment.

"Not one word," Niko says slowly and emphatically.

***

Their arrival at the cottage is not filled with the gleeful excitement that is usually the case. There is still a lot of acrimony simmering under the surface and it is impossible not to notice.

As they unpack the car and set up their rooms, very little is spoken until finally, Ashley can't bear the silence any longer.

"So she's an ex-girlfriend, big deal! We all have exes. It doesn't mean we can't still go and enjoy free lobster and red wine."

"Red wine with seafood? Really, Ashley?" Louie says as he passes by, allowing the condescending tone to linger in the air.

"Easy, we just don't go," Jeff says as he enters the cottage. "We just go on as if we never received the invitation."

"We can't not go," Niko insists. "Thanks to Chatty Cathy opening her big mouth, if we don't show up now it's going to look like this was a whole big deal."

"Which clearly it's not," Ashley mutters under her breath.

"I think we should go," Louie says.

"You think Niko would look bad if he bailed?" Jeff asks.

"Who cares about that? If there are some big shot muckety-mucks going, I might be able to get some inside information on the truth behind the Honey Harbour Honeys."

"Louie, for the last time, it's not a real thing," Niko says.

***

Niko's exasperation comes from the fact that ever since Louie first heard the legend of the Honeys, he's been obsessed with proving that it's true. This has been going on for decades. In fact, the reason Niko got up and pretended to be Beth's boyfriend on the pub patio 18 years earlier was because Louie was droning on about the Honey Harbour Honeys.

As the legend goes...in the early days of ship travel through the Georgian Bay ports, there was competition to bring the ships through the various ports. Merchant ships were the lifeblood of shop owners and craftspeople in those areas and steady ship traffic could mean the difference between riches and poverty.

To entice ships to stop in Honey Harbour, there were a group of 'hostesses' who would entertain the sailors when they came to town.

Of course, this posed a moral dilemma for the more pious townsfolk who relied on the ship traffic but could not abide by the methods used to ensure their continued visits.

So in time, the entire operation went underground. On the surface, no such activity could be seen taking place, so everyone was happy. But for those in the know, the Honeys could still be located, and their services still accessed.

Over time, ship traffic became less important and the Honeys were rendered obsolete by Father Time. But it is rumored that the Honey Harbour Honeys still exist to this day. And just as a Leprechaun must give up his pot of gold, anyone who successfully locates the Honey Harbour Honeys will find a sensual treasure as his reward.

Louie is determined to be that man.

***

Jeff has been around angry Niko enough to know there is no reasoning with him and the best course of action is to leave him alone and let him calm down on his own. So with Louie on the hunt for mythical creatures, Jeff and Ashley find themselves alone walking along the shoreline.

"I've never seen a woman have that kind of effect on him," Ashley says.

"You weren't around for the Beth experience. It was quite an ordeal."

"I'm kind of envious in a way."

"What could you possibly be envious of?" Jeff asks.

"I don't think I've ever been with someone who holds that kind of power over me all these years later. When they were together, it must have been incredible."

"They had chemistry, there was no denying that."

"Did you and Ellen have that kind of chemistry?"

Jeff doesn't answer right away. This question throws him for a bit. "We must have had something. We couldn't have stayed together for 20 years without anything at the core of it."

They walk in silence for another few moments.

"So how did he screw it up? What local skank did she find him with?"

Jeff just smiles. "You think that's what happened?"

Late Summer 2000

As the summer drew to a close, a feeling of dread was overcoming both Niko and Beth. Within days, the clock will strike midnight on this summer paradise and the demands and rigors of regular life will take over.

One of their favorite things to do is take a boat trip to Kennedy Island, a small island north of Honey Harbour. There are a handful of cottages on the island but a large chunk of it is uninhabited. They like to climb to the top of the island, lay on a blanket together and watch the stars after the sunset.

On this one late August night, Beth can't avoid the conversation any longer.

"I don't want to go," she said out of the blue.

"We can stay here for as long as you want."

"No, I mean Wisconsin. I don't think I can go."

"You have to go. You have a full ride swim scholarship to a Big Ten school. Do you have any idea what kind of opportunity that is?"

"I don't care. I just want us to be together."

Niko smiles as he looked into her eyes. "I know. I feel the same. But you'd be crazy not to go."

"God, you sound just like my father."

"He must be a smart man."

"Or maybe you're both just really old."

"Okay, I know this is going to make me sound really old but...you're only 18. You have the next four years ahead of you which will be one of the best times of your life. Dorm parties, swim competitions, new friends, the whole thing. It's a part of growing up that you need to embrace."

"Will we try the long distance thing?"

Niko chuckles. "I know in theory that works, but in reality, it almost never does. Look, I've seen it a million times. The pretty girl with the boyfriend back home has the best of intentions but she meets cute guys in the caf, or in class, or at a party and in time, the loneliness becomes too much to bear. They usually wake up in the cute guy's dorm room one morning, wracked with guilt and shame and then they have to call the boyfriend back home to have the talk."

"How do you know that's what happens?"

"Because I'm usually the guy they cheat with." This brings the slightest grin to Beth's face but was still not enough to remove her sadness. "I know it sucks, it sucks for me too. But we'll be together next summer. It will come around in no time."

"It won't feel like it."

"You'll be fine. I mean, it's not like you're in love with me," Niko said matter-of-factly.

Beth looked up with tears streaming down her face as she nods to contradict him, not agree with him.

This time, Niko is left completely speechless. He can only hold her in silence.

***

Upon arriving at the Secord cottage party, the first thing Ashley notices is how incredibly underdressed she is for the event. Even with her best summer top paired with her dressiest shorts and strappy sandals, she is still outshone by the elegant and expensive summer dresses that most of the women appear to be wearing.

She tells herself she will forgive Niko for this one day, but that day isn't coming anytime soon.

As she makes her way to the bar, Jeff and Louie find a table where they sit down and scope out the place. Jeff is simply trying to remain inconspicuous, hoping they all get through the night without any major incidents. Louie, however, has other plans.

He is convinced that someone at the party knows something that will help him in his quest for the elusive Honey Harbour Honeys. Just as he looks to see where he should situate himself, a conversation walks within his earshot.

"...taking the boat next week over to Mermaid Island," a man's voice is heard saying.

"Mermaid Island. I know why you want to go there," another man teases.

"Now, now. It's not like that."

"Hey, I'm not your wife. You don't have to put up a front with me."

The men move out of earshot but that's all Louie needed to hear.

"Mermaid Island! Of course!" Louie cries out, drawing the attention of those in the general area.

Mermaid Island is another small island in the Georgian Bay located west of Pleasant Point and east of Minnehaha Point and Royal Island. The guys have heard the name plenty of times, but only now does the name have any significance.

"What are you talking about?" Jeff asks.

"Why do you think they called it Mermaid Island? Mermaids... luring sailors...the Honey Harbour Honeys...it fits perfectly."

"I'm pretty sure you're thinking of sirens. Isn't the island shaped like a mermaid?"

It is and Jeff's logic was irrefutable to anyone not named Louie Delulio.

"I know I'm right. I've got to find out more."

"You have fun. I'm going to see if I can track down Ashley." Jeff says.

"It won't take long, she's over there talking to some GQ looking dude."

"What dude?" Jeff's head snaps around and, to his dismay, Louie was actually right this time. There, under a colored light, is Ashley laughing and chatting with a handsome, square-jawed man around their age. Whatever they're talking about, she seems to be enjoying the conversation.

Jeff can't look, but can't look away either.

On the other side of the property, Beth approaches Niko with two glasses of champagne. "I wasn't sure you'd come."

"You see, there's a sentence I've never said to a woman," he says, accepting a glass.

Beth bursts out laughing and then gently shakes her head as she looks deep into his eyes. "It's really you."

"You look great. Time's been a friend," Niko says softly.

"The same goes for you."

"Sure, but was that ever really in question?"

"You're an asshole."

"The place looks the same. Does your dad still have the boat?"

"Yep, same one. We had a lot of good times on that boat."

"A few of them even involved sailing."

"You remember?"

How could I forget? All those times we told your dad we were going down to the Marina to 'Prep the vessel.'" Niko says, emphasizing the air quotes.

"We prepped that vessel all night long sometimes."

"Yes, we did," Niko says.

A few moments of silence hang in the air before..."Do you think you might want to prep the vessel again?" Beth blurts out.

Niko is dumbstruck. Did she just say that? Is she serious?

Before he can get answers to any of his internal questions, Ashley's handsome GQ guy appears, putting his arm around Beth's waist. He kisses her on the cheek.

"Oh hi, hun," Beth says. "Have you met Niko? Niko this is my husband Matt."

They shake hands. "We actually met briefly many years ago," Matt says. "I hope I'm not interrupting anything."

"No, not at all," Niko spits out. "We were just talking about sailing."

Matt frowns ever so slightly. "That's too bad. I was hoping you were discussing the possibility of fucking my wife."

CHAPTER FOURTEEN

The following morning Jeff is awakened by the sound and smell of bacon sizzling in the frying pan. For his entire life, Jeff has prided himself on his ability to sleep on the horns of a yak. He's slept through thunderstorms and seismic tremors. But bacon? Bacon is a force too powerful for even Jeff.

To Jeff's delight, he finds Niko alone in the kitchen cooking enough food for either a small army or large religious cult. This is the first time he's seen Niko after his mysterious disappearance at Beth's parents' party. When things get weird, Niko tends to clam up. So extracting any information as to what happened would require a deft touch.

"What the hell happened to you last night?" Jeff spits out.

Okay, what it lacked in subtlety, it made up for in directness.

"Just had to get out of there," Niko says while tending to his scrambled eggs.

"Did something happen with Beth?"

"I really don't want to talk about it."

The thought occurs to Jeff that it doesn't seem that long ago when Jeff was fleeing an uncomfortable situation at his high school reunion and Niko was the first one to try to get him to talk about it. Now Niko is in full flight from whatever happened at that party and, at the risk of enraging Niko even further, Jeff needs to be there for him.

"Whatever it is, I'm sure I can help," Jeff offers in a calm, soothing voice.

Niko drops his spatula and spins on his heel. "Oh really! Okay then, 'Sage-of-the-mountain,' tell me what I should do about Beth's husband asking me to have sex with his wife?"

Jeff just stares at Niko, mouth agape. He thought he had heard it all when it came to girl-trouble, but that is one he was not expecting. "Wait, Beth is into the orgy scene?"

"We prefer to call it *The Lifestyle*," Beth's voice drifts in through the screen door. Neither Jeff nor Niko had noticed her arrival about a minute earlier.

"And it's not an *orgy scene*...well, at least not most times."

Flailing his arms, Jeff tries to dig himself out of it. "No, no, of course. I didn't mean to suggest th-"

"It's okay, Jeff. It's weird for most people at first. It takes some-- hey, is that freshly cooked bacon?" Walking in, Beth grabs a piece right out of the pan. "Mmmmm. Niko, you always made the best hangover breakfast."

"Did you come over just to steal my breakfast?" Niko asks.

"Not just that. You seemed pretty freaked out so I thought I'd come by and see if you wanted to go for a sail around the harbour. It would give us a little privacy so I could explain about last night."

Niko considers it for a few moments. "Okay."

"Great, now let's go prep the vessel," she says with a wink. "And I mean actually prepping the sailboat so don't get any ideas, perv."

"You're taking cottagers three at a time and I'm the perv?" Niko mutters to himself.

***

No matter how stressed they got, or how many troubles seemed to be weighing on their shoulders, for Niko and Beth, a day on the water made it all melt away. If the weirdness of the previous night was the ultimate test of the magical soothing powers of the water, the first 15 minutes of this adventure has left no room for doubt – Niko was back in his happy place.

Despite the awkward conversation and the fact that Beth is now a married woman, being in the boat with her one more time makes him feel 23 again. He forgot how much he missed that feeling.

But is it any different than it was before? There always seems to be something standing in the way.

Beth must have been reading his mind at that exact moment. "It's never simple for us, is it?"

"So how long?" Niko asks, impatient to get into the conversation that can no longer be avoided. "How long have you been in 'the lifestyle?'

"About five years. He's been wanting to get into it for the last 10 or 12 but I resisted."

"Why did you finally give in?"

"Two reasons. Our marriage had been struggling and we were drifting further and further apart with each passing month. I didn't know if we were going to make it. Odd as it sounds, I honestly thought it might be something that could bring us back together."

"I'm sure saving his marriage was his big motivation too," Niko says with more than a hint of sarcasm.

"No, he just wants to have sex with a lot of strangers. He is what we call 'spicy'; I am more vanilla."

"You don't want to be a part of it?"

Beth smiles as she ponders the answer to that question. "Maybe I should say I'm vanilla with sprinkles."

"So what was the other reason you agreed to it?"

"I found you on Facebook." This is the second time in less than 24 hours that Beth has rocked Niko with one simple sentence. She lets it hang in the air for a moment before continuing. "Everybody has a different way to practice 'the lifestyle.' Some couples like to go to clubs, meet another fun couple, drink, dance, then go upstairs and swap. Others prefer house parties with a trusted group of like-minded adults and have fun that way. Matt just wants to fuck as many different women as he possibly can."

"And you?"

"I don't want to sleep with a bunch of men outside of my marriage. I want to sleep with one man outside of my marriage."

"If it's not me, this is a serious dick move on your part," Niko says.

"Of course it's you, you massive tool! The only reason I agreed to let him explore the lifestyle the way he wants is so one day I could get a chance to explore it the way I want."

Niko doesn't say anything right away. This is a lot for him to take in and process.

"Matt has the kids tomorrow night. Let's sneak away for that overnight trip to Kennedy Island."

Niko's head turns swiftly. She has clearly struck a nerve. "Kennedy Island? You really want to bring that up?"

July 2004

When they parted ways at the end of the summer of 2000, Niko was genuine when he said they would pick up where they left off. That following summer, he could hardly wait for Beth to come back to Honey Harbour and tell him all about her first year at university. But as one of the star athletes in the swim program, she was selected to run one of the elite swim camps for high school kids throughout the summer.

Beth never made it back at all that summer or in any of the subsequent summers during her time as a Wisconsin Badger. Niko had given up on seeing her again until one day in the summer of 2004 when he saw a familiar face getting ice cream down by the waterfront.

"Do you go to university around here?" Niko asks before she could see him. Beth us startled but her eyes grow wide and she can't fight back a smile.

"I just graduated actually."

"From university? You graduated from university?"

"Yes, I graduated from university."

"I had to clarify that. You may find this hard to believe, but some young women can be quite sneaky."

Beth had decided to spend the summer at her parents' cottage and it doesn't take long for Niko and Beth to fall back into blissful familiar patterns. If there were ever a concern that it wouldn't be as good as that magical first summer together, that notion is quickly dismissed.

In fact, Niko feels like it was even better now. For one thing, he is now 27 and she's 22. He has five years of teaching under his belt and dating the Superintendent's 22-year-old college graduate daughter seems far less scandalous.

One weekend they decide to camp overnight on Kennedy Island. Their last visit there was less than joyous and they want to create more beautiful memories in their favorite secret getaway spot.

The evening they were supposed to leave, Niko us on the pier loading up the boat and waiting for Beth to arrive. He waits...and waits...and...waits. This is still two years before Beth would get her first cell phone, so he had no way to reach her.

She never shows.

***

"The next time I saw you, you were engaged to Matt," Niko says.

"I explained what happened!" Beth insists.

"I don't think you did."

"Because you wouldn't let me. But we can sit here and rehash that all again or we can enjoy ourselves and finally take that trip."

"Your husband is really okay with this?"

"It's the cost of doing business for him to get what he wants. And he gets off on it. Part of the deal is I have to give him a full account, blow-by-blow...so to speak."

Niko thinks about it for a while. But if there were any true doubt, it evaporated the second he looks deep into her eyes.

"Okay."

"Great. There's just one thing you have to do first," she says.

***

The Niko-Beth afternoon boat cruise was sure to be the talk of the cottage upon his return. One person who is completely out of the loop is Louie, who is totally oblivious to the day's drama.

About an hour before Jeff woke up and Beth arrived at Niko's cottage, Louie set out on an amorous adventure of his own. Ever since he overheard the conversation referencing Mermaid Island, Louie has been obsessed with going there.

Today, he woke up feeling like a kid on Christmas morning. Assuming, of course, that kid is a balding, middle-aged man with chronic back pain who's hoping to have group sex with a yet-to-be-proven, semi-mythical band of lake nymphs.

Regardless, he couldn't wait to head out on Niko's speedboat and be the one to find the Honey Harbour Honeys. Louie would be the first to admit he could be, if not gullible, highly impressionable. When Louie was a kid, he was certain he found Gremlins in his basement, only to discover he had been playing in a rat's nest. And years later, before the scam became cliché, Louie truly believed he had just bought into a Nigerian Prince's frozen fortune.

But this time, it's different. He can feel it. He knows it to be true. There are Honey Harbour Honeys and he's going to find them on Mermaid Island.

Louie's early attempts prove unsuccessful, but he chalks that up to failings in his approach. As it turns out, the high school Bible camp tour doesn't react well to the question, "Hey, does anyone know where I can find the whores?"

He got a better response when he asked locals if he could find 'entertainment' on the island. Better doesn't mean any actual information, just fewer people attempting to perform an exorcism on him.

Little did Louie know that like the parable of the good farmer who carefully planted seeds, his queries were about to bear fruit.

"Are you the guy looking for local entertainment?" a female voice asks.

The question instantly brought life to a previously sullen Louie who has been holding his head in his hands on a park bench. "Yes! Yes, I am."

"Would I be correct in assuming you are a gentleman interested in some group entertainment?"

"Yes."

"You'll have to speak to our leader, but I think you've found what you are looking for."

Louie is thrilled beyond belief. He isn't sure if it is because he was about to be proven right when everyone told him he was being foolish, or because he finally gets to utter his next sentence.

"Take me to your leader."

Louie follows the woman on a ten-minute walk inland. Eventually, they come to a residence where Louie is escorted inside. When he looks up, his eyes grow wide.

"No fucking way!"

***

Niko finds it slightly amusing that Matt wanted to meet on the same pub patio where Niko first met Beth almost 20 years earlier. He finds it downright eerie when he finds Matt sitting at the same table. Of course, he would soon find out that 'weird' would be the operative word for what was about to happen.

The two men shake hands and sit across from each other. They order a round of beers and wait for the server to leave.

"I'll bet you thought I was messing with you," Matt says with a sly grin.

"I hadn't ruled out a hidden camera practical joke show."

"This is no joke, I assure you," Matt says. "I understand Beth has told you about our marital arrangement."

"Yes, I heard all about 'the lifestyle'. But there's one thing I don't get."

"What's that?"

"If it's a longstanding arrangement, what am I doing here? Surely, I don't need to ask your permission."

"Not ask permission. To provide assurance. The lifestyle works because it's about physical intimacy, not emotional intimacy. When the night is over, everyone goes back to their own spouse in their own house. No happy homes are disrupted. But you and Beth have a past. And I get that she's more comfortable exploring this with someone she trusts. But I need to trust that you have no ulterior motives here."

For someone who loves irony as much as he does, the sweetness of this moment is about to send Niko into a diabetic coma. This is the Bizarro World version of a conversation he's had a million times before. Normally he has to give assurances that he's not trying to sleep with someone's wife. Of course, most of the time, he's lying.

If you did an actuary table for Niko's most likely cause of death given his pattern of behavior, despite the long and steady history of heart disease in the Stassinopoulos family, it would still lag miles behind the number one likelihood – shot by a jealous husband.

So just as Louie got to say one of his all-time favorite sentences, Niko was about to utter one of his.

"I assure you, on my honor, I just want to fuck your wife."

Matt smiles. "Glad to hear it."

Niko starts to get up but Matt puts his hand on Niko's arm. "Just one more thing and I hate to do this but it is a deal-breaker."

Please don't want to watch. Please don't want to watch. Please don't want to watch. Niko kept repeating it in his head. He was terrified to ask. "And what is that?"

"Tell me about your friend Ashley."

***

"Boys, I'm throwing a party!" Louie is so excited, he doesn't really notice that Jeff, Ashley, and Niko seemed preoccupied and don't really react to his announcement. "Tomorrow night, the Honey Harbour Honeys will be showing up here."

This is enough to somewhat grab their attention.

"What?" Jeff asks.

"I can't say who I talked to or why I know as I was sworn to secrecy but...don't be surprised when I am bathed in honey all night long."

The three reacted with understandable disgust. The image was distasteful by any objective standard. Ashley suddenly stands and heads for the door. "I have to go for a walk."

"Geez, what's with Miss Priss all of a sudden?" Louie asks.

If he were significantly less self-absorbed and better equipped to read the room, Louie would have suspected that he had arrived back at the cottage at an inopportune time.

Just twenty minutes earlier, Niko briefed Jeff and Ashley on his meeting with Matt and how Ashley's participation is conditional to it all happening.

Ashley was trying to sort out how she felt about being thrown into the mix. On one hand, she was flattered to be the object of affection of such a handsome man. And while she wanted to help Niko and Beth rekindle their spark, the quid pro quo aspect made her feel a bit like a prostitute. And not the 'never-kiss-on-the-mouth elegant *Pretty Woman'* kind. More like the truck-stop $15 BJ kind.

Matt suspected she might feel that way, and told Niko to stress that he only wants a date - as in, the pleasure of her company, with no demand or expectation of sex. This, of course, begs the question of which is the more mythical character – The Honey Harbour Honey or the chaste swinger?

***

Whether or not he knew why, Jeff finds himself running out the door after Ashley. It could have been as simple as making sure a friend was okay or there may have been something more to it. His first question may have been more revealing than he expected.

"You're not going to go through with it, are you?" he said, half out of breath after jogging to catch up.

Ashley just looks at Jeff before responding to his seemingly abrupt question. She looks at him like they were head to head at the final table of the World Series of Poker. She is looking for a tell before she plays her hand.

"You don't think I should help out Niko?"

It was a trick question and Jeff could sense the trap. Of course, one should help out a friend, but not if it means...not if it just doesn't feel right. "It's not that."

Ashley takes a few steps towards him. "Well then what is it, Jeff? What do you want me to do?"

"I don't know."

"Don't think about it. Tell me what your gut says. Deep down, can you come up with a reason why I shouldn't go on a date with Matt?"

Jeff is speechless.

"It just doesn't feel right in my gut."

That wasn't exactly the answer she was looking for but it wasn't the wrong answer either. It was a definite maybe which doesn't make anything clearer for her.

"But I'm torn because I hated the way Niko and Beth ended it," Jeff adds.

August 2004

A week have passed since Beth left Niko standing on the pier when they were supposed to get away to Kennedy Island. Niko is now coming in from an evening boat cruise around the harbour and when he pulls up to the dock, he sees Beth standing there, waiting for him.

Two things were immediately noticeable upon first glance: first, she looks contrite. You can tell she was unsure how he would receive her.

The other is the sparkle of the diamond ring catching the reflection of the setting sun. She doesn't even have to utter a word and Niko has all he needs to know about what happened. He didn't need the gory details.

He kills the engine, ties up the boat and steps onto the dock. "It looks like congratulations are in order," he offers with mock enthusiasm.

"I guess so."

"You know, you could have told me."

"I didn't know."

"You didn't know you got engaged to be married?"

"I didn't know this was happening at all. Matt planned it all with my parents. He had the whole thing set up for the night we were supposed to go to the island. I didn't even know he was coming up. He said he wanted it to be a surprise."

"Surprise!"

"I wanted to tell you right away. I needed you to know I would never knowingly leave you hanging like this. But I also wanted to give you time to cool off."

He looks at her for a few moments. "So that's it then?"

"That's it," she says matter-of-factly.

"Well, Mazel Tov. I wish you both the very best."

Niko walks off and casts one last glance over his shoulder where he sees Beth shaking her head, laughing. She had always said she finds it funny when Niko gets in one of his huffs.

This one, she must have found hilarious.

***

"That was the last time he saw her before this weekend," Jeff says.

"That does explain why he was so pissed at me when I invited us all to her place that night," Ashley says, as they both sit on lawn chairs looking out over the water. "It's like they could just never the get the timing right."

"Yeah, timing's everything it seems."

"Still, it's amazing how those feelings stay strong all those years later," Ashley says.

"I like to think when it's right, those feelings will always be there, no matter how much time has gone by. Don't you?" Jeff says.

Ashley is speechless. Was Jeff trying to say something? She replies with a simple "I do."

Then a thought strikes her, and a smile creeps across her face.

"Do you think it would still count for Niko and Beth if I agreed to a lunch date? He might think there is more, but it would be just lunch. What do you think of that idea?"

Jeff smiles, "I think that would work...for everyone."

***

The following night while Louie is taking care of the final touches for his big party, Niko is getting the boat ready for the trip to the island when he sees Beth making her way towards the boat.

"Scale of one to ten, how shocked are you that I showed up," she says.

"One," he says without a moment's hesitation.

"One? You didn't have any doubt at all?"

"You're already married. He can't propose again." She laughs. "Come on, let's grab the rest of the supplies from the place before Louie infests it with his Louieness."

Niko's arm is around Beth's waist as they walk up to the cottage. To the casual observer, their past is all water under the bridge. But as they near the cottage, Niko looks up and sees something that gives him a reaction, not unlike Jeff's reaction upon first laying eyes on Beth.

"Oh shit!"

"What?" Beth asks.

There, on the front deck talking and laughing with Louie is Jeff's ex, Ellen.

"Beth, I can't go to the Island."

Tony Sekulich

CHAPTER FIFTEEN

When the boys were in University, they lived right around the corner from a chicken and burger fast food place called *The Cluck & Chuck*. It was convenient and cheap, pretty much the only two things that matter to the not-so-discerning palate of a university student. So you would think that the place would have been a second home for the guys but the truth is, they never spent a lot of time there.

The first time they went, the chicken was still half frozen, the burgers were charred and the fries were greasy enough to be considered a genuine fire hazard. Needless to say, they didn't return anytime soon.

But about a year later Niko found himself walking by the place and thinking, 'the Cluck & Chuck, I haven't been there in ages. I should pop in and give it a try.' He went in, ordered the same thing as the previous year, and two bites in, it struck him. 'THIS is why I haven't been here in ages'.

Niko would repeat this process once a year, like clockwork. He probably ate there a dozen times in his life. Each visit, as unpleasant as the one that came before. The repeated visits were not because Niko is some kind of gastro-sadist. It's because the brain has a way of blocking out or glossing over unpleasant experiences from the past. This then creates a false sense of nostalgia for the good ole days that were rarely anything close to being good.

So when Niko looked up at his front deck and saw Ellen chatting and laughing it up with Louie, he saw the one person who caused his best friend the most agony and misery he ever experienced in the entirety of his lifetime.

But he also knew when Jeff laid eyes on her, he would see something completely different. Jeff would see The Cluck & Chuck.

"What the fuck is she doing here," Niko says as he not-so-subtly drags Louie by the collar to an unoccupied corner of the deck.

"You are not going to believe this," Louie says, too excited about what he was finally able to reveal.

"I already don't believe it," Niko says.

"Ellen is the leader of the Honey Harbour Honeys!"

"I stand corrected. That goes light years beyond unbelievable and has landed squarely into are-you-out-of-your-fucking-mind territory."

"I'm telling you, it's all true. The other day when I went to Mermaid Island....

Flashback to Mermaid Island

"No fucking way!"

Louie wasn't sure what to expect when he was taken on a mysterious trek to find the leader of the Honey Harbour Honeys. If he were being honest with himself, he was really hoping it would be one of his favorite SI swimsuit edition cover models Paulina Porizkova, Kathy Ireland, or Elle MacPherson.

Being pleasured by a group of hyper-sexualized lake-nymphs led by one of his boyhood fantasy women would just be karma for all the haters who said he was on a fool's errand. A modern day Don Quixote with a pharmaceutically enhanced erection.

But as unlikely as this was of coming true, it would have still seemed far more likely than discovering Jeff's ex-wife standing there waiting to greet him.

"Hi, Louie!"

"Ellen, what are you doing here?"

"I've been coming here for years, you know that."

Now that she mentioned it, he does recall something about Ellen going up to visit her cousin somewhere in cottage country. For the last five years of their marriage, Ellen and Jeff would routinely take separate cottage trips to the same general area. Jeff would do the Canada Day boys trip while Ellen would do crafts and wine tasting with her cousin. Or at least that's the best guess Louie could muster. When Jeff would tell him where Ellen was going and what she was doing, Louie filed all that information in the part of his brain labeled 'stuff Louie doesn't care about'.

So what came out of his mouth next could kindly be considered a performance, but more accurately described as complete horseshit. "Don't be silly. Of course, I remember. How could I forget?"

"I understand you're here looking for...entertainment," Ellen offers cautiously.

"Yes, I am!"

"Am I correct in assuming you are looking for group entertainment?"

"You could be," Louie says.

"Well, I think my girls are exactly what you're looking for."

"You have a group of girls?" Louie can barely contain his excitement.

"They haven't failed to please yet. I think they are exactly what you've come looking for."

"Are they here?" Louie is seconds away from ripping off his shirt right there on the spot.

"No, they aren't here. They go to you. Are you having a party at Niko's cottage this weekend?"

"Yes, as a matter of fact, we are. Two nights from now."

"My girls and I will be there."

***

"Remember me?"

The sound of her voice went right through Jeff like a bolt of lightning. He turned around to see Ellen and he froze. He wasn't terrified, he wasn't thrilled, he was just paralyzed.

"Well don't just stand there. Give me a hug." Ellen goes up to him and throws her arms around him. Jeff reciprocates more out of obligation than genuine affection.

"Ellen, wow! What..." he couldn't find a polite way to finish the sentence.

"What am I doing here? Louie invited me."

Ashley decides to sidle up and join this impromptu reunion. Jeff doesn't notice that Ashley is there and it falls on Ellen to introduce herself. She offers Ashley her hand.

"Hi, I'm Ellen."

Ashley shakes her hand. "Ashley."

Just the one word was enough to trigger something in Ellen's memory. There is something very familiar in Ashley's look and the sound of her voice, but she can't quite place it. "Have we met before?"

Ashley is now horrified as the memory of the only time they crossed paths comes rushing back. The night of the high school reunion when Ashley was charged with the task of distracting Ellen.

"I love this material. It's so soft."

"Thank you," Ellen says cautiously.

"It looks great on you. It really compliments your figure. God, you have such a great body."

"No, I don't think we have," Ashley says, praying her nose won't grow five inches right there on the spot.

Ellen turns her attention back toward Jeff. "You look really good."

"Thanks," he says sheepishly.

"Have you been working out? Are you eating vegan?" Ellen asks sincerely.

Ashley scoffs just a little louder than what she intended. Ellen and Jeff look at her.

"Oh, you were serious?" Ashley says.

"No, I haven't been working out, not eating vegan, but I have been trying new things."

"Did I hear you're coaching a girls basketball team?"

"That's true. I just started last month. They don't have a lot of natural talent but they make up for it by really detesting their coach."

Ellen laughs, a bit too much for Ashley's liking.

"I've been trying new things, taking on new adventures all in an attempt to become the new Jeff Dempsey. I'm even vlogging about it."

"Really? Jeff Dempsey with a vlog? It's hard to imagine."

"It's true."

"Well I have to say, it's really working for you."

There is something in that comment that really puts Jeff at ease. What defenses he had up are suddenly dropped. It's been forever since he can recall seeing Ellen this pleasant and personable. It reminds him of how they were when they first got together.

"Thank you!" he says.

"So no personal trainer, no home chef, you've been doing this all by yourself?" Ellen asks.

She couldn't have teed it up any better for Jeff to give Ashley her due. Anyone who's been around Jeff since the high school reunion knows he would have remained lost without Ashley. False modesty aside, Ashley knows it too. Which is why what happened next was all the more painful.

"Yep, it's a solo journey. I get up every day and try to do one thing the old me was too afraid to do."

Not giving her credit is one thing. Snubbing her while stealing the mantra she came up with is entirely too much for her to take right now. Ashley rushes out of the cottage, afraid she's going to either burst into tears or a murderous rage.

***

"Is there a Louie here?"

The voice has a seasoned, husky tone to it. This is clearly not the voice of a young ingénue or delicate wilting flower. No, as soon as he hears it, Louie knows the woman to whom that voice belongs has experience. She's been around long enough to see a thing or two in her day. He hasn't yet turned around to confirm but he doesn't have to. In his gut, he knows he's right.

What he doesn't know is just how right he is.

He turns around and before he can say anything, four women aged 70 and up break out into a song and dance performance of "The Boogie Woogie Bugle Boy of Company B."

He has to blink and shake his head to be certain his eyes aren't deceiving him. They can all sing, there is nothing wrong with the performance. But as he goes from one singer to the next, each one looks that much closer to death than the one before. It is as if *Pitch Perfect* is being performed by the Crypt Keeper's grandmothers.

When it ends, the performance draws a smattering of applause from those nearby. One person who is not applauding is Louie, who is still too stunned to process what has just happened.

"What the fuck is this?" Louie exclaims.

"We're the entertainment you asked for," says Nancy, the lead singer. "We're the Honey Harbour Hollies."

And in that moment, Louie discovers that like a lot of urban legends, there is often a kernel of truth surrounded by bullshit. In this case, the Honey Harbour Hollies have been around entertaining men for decades. Just not in the way Louie had hoped.

***

Niko finds Ashley collecting herself in a secluded area down by the water. He walks up to her and puts his hand on her shoulder. "Are you okay?"

"Why do I keep doing this to myself?" Ashley asks rhetorically. "Just when I think I have my shit together, it's like I take six steps back."

"I know you don't want to hear this, but you have to go tell him how you feel. Right now."

"He doesn't want to hear it from me."

"He doesn't know he wants to hear it from you. And he's never going to know if he keeps spending time with that succubus in my kitchen."

"Why do you care? Shouldn't you be out sticking it to a married woman...again?"

"I know I allowed the Beth thing to get in the way of my plans to get you and Jeff together, but it's not too late for you. Don't let that window close on you."

"Oh please! What do you know about closing windows?"

"More than anyone really should," he says as he walks away.

Ashley considers what he says and she knows he's not totally wrong, but there is no way she can face Jeff after what he just did to her.

"He's right, you know." The voice startles Ashley and she turns to see that Beth has joined her.

"You heard us?" Ashley asks.

"I heard enough. And I've seen the way you look at him. I know that look well. I've worn it more than a few times in the last 17 years."

"How did you know when it was time to move on?"

"I was hoping you could tell me," Beth says.

"I mean, that time on the dock just after you got engaged when you told Niko that it was over for good."

"Is that what you think happened?"

August 2004

Beth gives Ashley her account of what happened that last night Niko and Beth saw each other. The day they were supposed to leave for the island was filled with a mix of excitement and dread for Beth. She couldn't wait to take that getaway trip with Niko but she couldn't shake the feeling that something bad was about to happen.

First off, her family was acting extremely weird that whole weekend. They usually didn't micro-manage her time but suddenly they had to know where she was and what she was doing every minute of the day.

Her older sister insisted on taking Beth on a nature hike to Jordan's Lookout, one of the more scenic hiking trails in the area. It was where she and Matt first went when they decided to be exclusive with each other. So when she reached the lookout and found Matt down on one knee with a string quartet playing behind him, it should not have been a complete surprise.

Except it was.

She had never for a moment considered marrying Matt. They were fine as a couple but they fought quite a bit. At first, she thought it was just part of being in a relationship but when she looked around and saw that for most other couples, fights were the exception and not the default setting, she figured there must be something wrong.

And when she restarted her fling with Niko, she didn't really consider it cheating. In her mind Matt was her ex-boyfriend, she just hadn't gotten around to telling him that yet. He wasn't supposed to be here that weekend. And if she had any inkling this was coming, she would have put a stop to it before it got this far.

But here she is. Being proposed to by her would-be Prince Charming in front of her family members at Jordan's Lookout. What could she say? 'I think we should slow down and give this some thought. I'm not saying no but I definitely can't give you a yes right now. Calgon, take me away.'

Any of those would have been acceptable if they were alone. But right there, at that moment, in that situation, it appeared as if she had only one acceptable course of action.

"Yes!" she says as she holds out her left hand so Matt can slip on the ring.

The following week when she finally saw Niko, she was going to tell him everything. Why she had to bail on him and how she was trapped into accepting the proposal. But it didn't play out the way she hoped.

Beth recalls the conversation pretty much as Niko relayed it. With one important distinction.

***

"So it looks like congratulations are in order," Niko offered with mock enthusiasm.

"I guess so."

"You know, you could have told me."

"I didn't know."

"You didn't know you got engaged to be married?"

"I didn't know this was happening at all. Matt planned it all with parents. He had the whole thing set up for the night we were supposed to go to the island. I didn't even know he was coming up. He said he wanted it to be a surprise."

"Surprise!"

"I wanted to tell you right away. I needed you to know I would never knowingly leave you hanging. But I also wanted to give you time to cool off."

He looks at her for a few moments. "So...that's it then!" The statement is cold and matter-of-fact. No need to parse it for hidden meaning.

"That's it?" she asks in complete disbelief. How can he end things just like that?

"Well, Mazel Tov. I wish you both the very best."

Niko walks off and looks back one more time over his shoulder. Had he taken more than a cursory glance, he would have seen that Beth is not laughing at his rage, she is sobbing in her hands.

***

"God, he was so petulant and pig-headed. He acted like such a..." Beth can't come up with just the right word.

"...man?" Ashley offers. This brings a smile to Beth's face.

"Yes. Like a man. I didn't go to him that night to tell him I got engaged. I went to him to give me even the tiniest reason why I shouldn't go through with it."

"So why did you marry Matt?"

"I wish I could tell you. I think the engagement was just one of those things where once I did it, it got harder and harder to undo. I know one thing that would have put the brakes on it though."

"What's that?"

"If I had seen Niko on the day of my wedding, there's no way I would have gone through with it. We would have had a real-life runaway bride situation on our hands."

"Was he invited?"

"My parents wanted to invite all the cottagers to the wedding but I never sent his invitation. It's weird, I buried his invitation but I was still hoping he'd show up."

"He doesn't know any of this. He thinks you just threw him away. You have to go tell him!"

"If one of us had voiced our true feelings, who knows what could have happened. But I'm not the one who has to go tell a boy how I feel."

Sometimes those ghosts that we think are there to haunt us aren't scary ghosts at all. They're more like friendly spirits who help guide us and point us in the right direction when we find ourselves hopelessly lost.

"Go to him," Beth says emphatically. "Don't make my mistake. Don't let foolish pride keep you from voicing your truth."

***

Louie sits on the couch in Niko's cottage sullen and seemingly absent of any life or hope. His despair is evident to anyone who passes by.

"Why are you so sad?" Nancy asks as she sits down beside him.

"I was really hoping to find a group of lake nymphs who would reward me with unlimited sensual pleasures but it turns out they're not real."

"Acapella singers are horny AF," Nancy says. Louie's head snaps up. "Why do you think we do this? We need to get that sweet D."

Another comes by and sits down on Louie's other side. "Have you ever done a double century club?"

"What is it?" Louie asks with a trembling in his voice.

"It's like a three-way but when the combined age in the bed is at least 200."

Louie is intrigued...and a little horrified...but mostly intrigued.

***

Niko finds Beth out by the water. "I thought I'd find you here."

Whenever ghosts do appear, it is almost always to deliver a message.

"We're never going to take that trip to the Island, are we?"
"No, we're not," Niko says.

That message could be as simple as it's time to close a chapter in your heart."

"Being with you Beth is like drinking seawater," Niko continues. It doesn't quench that thirst and just leaves you desperate for more."

"I know."

They fall into each other's arms and hold each other tight for one last time.

Or they could manifest themselves in a ghastly physical appearance to punish the foolhardy for the ill-advised path they have chosen.

In Louie's bedroom, the geriatric Honey Harbour Hollies disrobe and are about to slip into Louie's bed. Just as the last item of clothing hits the floor, the clouds part and moonlight pours through the open window illuminating the Hollies in their full nakedness. For their age, the Hollies have held up fairly well and should be proud. However, for someone as shallow as Louie, the image is jarring and more than a little disturbing. "Nooooooooooooo!"

***

Ashley walks briskly around the cottage grounds looking for Jeff. She has looked almost everywhere but to no avail. It occurs to her that she had not checked the porch swing Niko set up behind the cottage. As she rounds the corner she can't decide if she wants to find him back here or not.

And sometimes you don't have to wait around and wonder when the ghosts will appear.

Ashley turns the corner and stops dead when she sees Jeff and Ellen cuddling and kissing on the swing. Ashley spins on her heel and walks away as tears stream down her face.

Because that exact moment when the opportunity dies is when they show up and the haunting begins.

Part Six

The Six-Month Backslide

Tony Sekulich

CHAPTER SIXTEEN

March 1995

Jeff Dempsey has that look.

It's one of those universal human expressions that we all instantly recognize. It's the look you would have after stepping in dog shit on the way into the most important job interview of your life. Or if you looked up to see the car you just rear-ended is a parked police cruiser.

It's an expression that encapsulates contempt, anger, frustration, and overall exasperation. And for the last 20 minutes, it has been permanently affixed to Jeff's 17-year-old baby face.

What caused this look is not necessarily anything he did or saw. Instead, his dismay is caused by something he heard...over and over and over again. It's the unmistakable sound that any basketball player dreads, the seemingly deafening sound of the ball CLANGING off the iron. Each time, echoing off the walls of the Holy Trinity High School gym.

He's fired up so many bricks, he's expecting someone to rush in and give him a well-earned Mason's union membership card.

Had he been searching for excuses, he wouldn't have to look too far. His plaid button-up long-sleeve shirt and faded blue-jeans are not exactly conducive to draining long jumpers. He hasn't had a proper warm-up given that he skipped third-period Religious Studies so he could get in 15 to 20 minutes of shooting as a confidence booster. As another shot ricochets off the rim and slams against the wall, he now sees the folly in this plan.

His only consolation is that he is suffering this humiliation alone. There is nobody else in the gym to bear witness to this Hindenburg of a shooting display.

"Your elbow is flying out."

Or so he thought.

The female voice was familiar although he couldn't immediately place it. Jeff turns around to see 15-year-old Ginny Holder, the varsity team's equipment manager, standing behind him. Two decades later, he would be re-introduced to her as Ashley but at that point in time, Jeff had no idea how their paths would cross again. Right now, she is just Ginny, the Grade 10 girl who makes sure the team's uniforms are ready for the games and the ball racks are out for pre-game warm up.

Her comment has Jeff perplexed and almost unsure where to begin. As adults, this is an occurrence that will become commonplace for him. But for now, Jeff is more than a little annoyed.

"What?" he offers as more of a statement than a question.

Ginny takes a few steps towards him. "Your shooting elbow is cocked way out to the side." Ginny mimics the shooting motion that has the shooting elbow pointed out at a 45-degree angle. She then brings it in so her forearm is more straight up and down. "This is how you normally shoot."

Jeff's delicate male ego makes him instantly resistant to taking shooting tips from a girl two years younger. On the other hand, he can't bear the sound of another missed shot so he's ready to try just about anything. Jeff picks up the ball, squares up to the basket, launches a jumper with his elbow in and...SWISH.

Dead. Solid. Perfect.

He looks at Ginny who does her best to hide a smug, satisfied grin. "Thanks, kid," he says in a cool-guy voice and starts to walk out of the gym. He doesn't realize he's being followed until he hears that voice again.

"You nervous about Franklin Heights tomorrow?"

"I don't get nervous," Jeff offers in his best Steve McQueen demeanor. Of course, that was total horseshit. As lies go, that is one of the top five he's ever told. It's right up there with, 'Of course, I'd love to see your slam poetry reading,' and 'Oh my God, you love Carrot Top movies too?!?'

Jeff nearly throws up before every game and the next day's Provincial Semi-Final will be the biggest game of his life. So while his guts will be twisted up six ways to Sunday, the team's geeky equipment manager doesn't need to know this.

"You're going to have a big game against Franklin Heights. I can just tell."

Jeff doesn't respond as he walks briskly down the first-floor hallway. Ginny follows right beside him.

"Why are you following me?" Jeff asks as politely as one can conceivably pose that question.

"We have chemistry," Ginny offers matter-of-factly.

This stops Jeff in his tracks. What did she just say? What did she mean by that? And while he doesn't voice those questions aloud, they are clearly plastered all over his face.

"Dr. Moore's 11-2 Chemistry. I'm in that class with you."

"Right, of course. We have chemistry," Jeff says.

***

When I was in high school, my favorite class was Dr. Moore's Chemistry class. He was one of the best teachers in the school and he always made learning fun. After high school, we became close friends and once a week, I'll visit with him in his retirement home.

One of the lessons that always stuck with me was when we were learning about litmus tests. Dr. Moore told us to appreciate litmus paper as being one of the rare things in life that is without nuance. At the time, nobody really understood what he meant. I think he knew that too because he said, "One day you'll appreciate the sheer simplicity of something that is either one thing or another."

Acid turns blue litmus paper red. Bases turn red litmus paper blue. That's it. There are no mitigating circumstances, no explanations, no exceptions. It's black and white...or I guess in this case, red and blue. A substance is either an acid or a base and there is no arguing with the results.

In real life, it seems everything is subjective or contextual. Even things we think we can take as givens are never as clear-cut as we'd like them to be. The sky is blue...except in certain circumstances when it can appear orange, purple, and sometimes bright red. So is the sky blue? Kind of, sort of, sometimes.

I've been thinking a lot lately about something Dr. Moore said at the end of that lesson. "Litmus tests are not relegated solely to the domain of the science lab. They are all around us. You just need to open our eyes and see them. And when you do, trust that they will never give you a false reading. That, my young friends, is scientifically impossible."

***

The silence is more than deafening. Normally, Sunday brunch at Jeff & Niko's apartment is abuzz with conversation and laughter, often at one of Louie's embarrassing misadventures.

But today is different. Not just because Louie is running late and it's just three of them waiting to dig into plates of steaming hot waffles. It's the 'who' that comprise 'the three' that has things completely out of whack. Seated around the table are Niko, Jeff, and Ellen, who is making her homemade Sunday brunch debut.

They will occasionally glance at their phones or reply to a text, but absent is anything that could generously be described as conversation. That is not to say that there was no speaking at all.

"Tell me again why we're not at one of the best King Street brunch spots," Ellen offers without a trace of bemusement.

Niko gives Jeff a sharp look that indicates this is Jeff's question to field.

"This is our Sunday thing. We get together, eat waffles, share stories. It's a tradition."

"Men owning women as property is a tradition. It doesn't mean we need to keep doing it," she says.

Niko is both clenching his fists and biting his lip. Something needs to give soon or he will explode. That 'something' takes the form of Louie who mopes through the door. Louie has never been the most dynamic person but even for him, it's not hard to tell something is amiss.

"Hey guys," he offers in much the same tone Eeyore would, had he downed a hoof-full of Quaaludes.

"What's wrong, Lou?" Jeff asks.

"I don't really want to talk about it."

"Are you okay?" Niko asks.

"It's a work thing. I kind of got fired," Louie offers.

"How do you kind of get fired?" Ellen asks seemingly more out of curiosity than genuine concern.

"By actually getting fired," Louie says.

Jeff goes over and sits beside him on the couch. "Can you tell us what happened?"

"I was put in charge of coordinating Mentoring Day. That's when high school students come in and they shadow someone in the office to learn what their career is all about. So in the invitation email that went out to all the schools, I mentioned how this would be a tremendous opportunity for them to get firsthand job experience in a real-world setting."

"Right, so what's the issue?" Jeff wonders.

"Well, instead of making 'first' and 'hand' one word, I left a space and made them two words."

It takes them a moment to piece it together. "So instead of offering them *firsthand job experience*, you promised a bunch of high school kids..."

"...their first hand job experience," Louie confirms.

The room explodes with laughter.

"Guys, it's not funny!"

Jeff is laughing so hard, he can barely breathe. "Sorry, Lou. I beg to differ."

The one person who does not find it uproariously funny is Ellen who is still a bit confused.

"It's an unfortunate mistake but hardly something to be fired over," she says.

"Wait, do we know for sure it's a mistake?" Niko says. "Is there a chance some of the mentors were actually going to give them their first handjob experience?"

Louie ignores this and turns to Ellen. "I was already on probation for inappropriate office conduct."

Ellen is even more puzzled.

Once again, Niko is only too happy to clarify. "He demanded his boss install glory holes in all the men's room stalls."

Jeff stands up and tries to get the day back on track. "Lady and gentlemen, may I propose we sit down and have brunch."

The group sits around the table and they start to load up their plates. Niko starts looking around. "I'm worried I'm going to get syrup on my pants. Lou, can you give me a handie...er, I mean hankie."

"Hey, leave him alone," Jeff says. "He's had a rough go but I'm sure this whole thing will have a happy ending."

Jeff and Niko laugh once more as Louie sits stone-faced. "Are you clowns done now?"

"Not even close!" Niko declares.

"Well maybe there will be change all around soon," Ellen says, clearly driving at something.

"What do you mean?" Jeff asks.

"Well, Louie's going to find a new job and soon you'll have a new place to live."

This last comment just sucked all the air out of the room. Niko and Louie exchange a WTF look. Even Jeff isn't sure what prompted this. Living with Niko at the age of 40 was never the plan but in the aftermath of Ellen leaving, their living situation has given Jeff some much needed calm and stability. It feels like home and while he doesn't envision them becoming the Sunshine Boys in their golden years, he doesn't see any reason to change things now.

"Why would I be finding a new place to live?"

"This has been great in a short-term pinch but, let's be honest, it's embarrassing for two middle-aged men to be living as roommates."

"Is it, now?" Niko says. "I was completely unaware of that. It's weird though because I'm not embarrassed. I'm fairly sure my buddy Jeff here isn't embarrassed. So I guess what I'm left wondering is, who exactly finds this embarrassing?"

Ellen glares at him but doesn't respond. The four put their heads down and eat brunch in silence.

***

Niko has been to Ashley's apartment more than a handful of times, but never has he felt more trepidation than at the current moment as he's about to knock on her door. And that is saying something considering not long ago, he almost burned the place down while having a secret forbidden tryst with one of her clients.

When Ashley opens the door and sees that it's Niko, it becomes clear that she is as unimpressed with his being there as he is. "Oh, it's you."

"I wasn't expecting a tearful leap into my arms, but I thought some genuine warmth would be nice."

His attempt to lighten the mood barely makes a dent. "What do you want, Niko?"

"Can we talk?"

After a few seconds of serious consideration, she opens the door and lets him in. It doesn't take two Sherpa guides and a bloodhound to root out the underlying cause of the tension. This is the first time the two have seen each other since the disastrous cottage weekend.

Everyone feels like their lives have been flipped upside down since those fateful days. It's like an alien body has infested their delicate ecosystem and thrown everything out of whack. And that alien's name is Ellen.

Niko takes a seat across from Ashley and they just look at each other in silence.

"How have you been?" Niko asks cautiously.

"What do you think?" Ashley fires back. Niko just nods knowingly. Ever since she saw Jeff and Ellen making out at the cottage, it's like she's been weighed down by this cloak of sadness that she just can't shake. "How's the happy couple?"

"I hate her. I hate her so much!"

This manages to bring the first trace of a smile to Ashley's face in what seems like forever.

"I know people say you shouldn't say you hate people, but I'm fairly certain those people have never met Ellen."

"Again, what do you want, Niko?"

"I want you to reach out to the boy."

"You know I can't do that."

"He really does need you. Now more than ever."

"But I can't be around him. I can't watch them be together. I'm actually thinking of moving away."

"Where would you go?"

"I don't know. I reinvented myself once, I can do it again."

"If you were your own life coach, is that what you would advise yourself? To run away."

"If we could be our own life coaches, none of us would be as messed up as we are."

"What if you two just happened to wind up at the same place at the same time?"

Ashley doesn't respond immediately which causes Niko to smile. If she were really dead set against it, she would have shot it down by now.

"Maybe," she says.

"That's all I needed to hear."

***

There are few places Jeff hates more than IKEA. When he's voiced this thought publicly, he usually draws the ire of many IKEAphiles whose idea of a day well spent is wandering through the store looking for their next piece of 'easy to assemble' furniture. But his loathing has nothing to do with the products or the degree of difficulty involved in assembling them. It's the store itself.

Jeff approaches shopping the same way Navy Seals approach POW extractions. Formulate a plan, then strike with precision. In and out before anyone realizes you're there. One of Jeff's proudest moments was when he completed his Christmas shopping in 15 minutes. After spending most of the day of the 23rd doing *recon*, he decided on the five presents he had to buy. After a series of surgical strikes, he was in the food court enjoying a vanilla latte in the blink of an eye.

This is the reason he hates IKEA. The floor plan design makes surgical strikes, impossible. The only way to get through the store is to make a day of it. Which is fine when you're an engaged young couple sorting out your registry. But when you are supposed to be meeting your friends for drinks, all you can think about is how you can get airlifted out.

"What do you think?" Ellen asks, snapping Jeff out of his helicopter fantasy. Jeff is trying to figure out how to answer given he has no idea what she's talking about. "The chair! What do you think of the chair? Would it look good in the den?"

Jeff has been here before. He knows there's a right answer and she's looking for confirmation of what she's already decided for herself. "It might, we'd really have to see it in the space."

"Yeah, I'm thinking it might clash with what's there already," she says.

Landmine averted.

Jeff checks the time on his phone and makes a face. "How much longer do you think we'll be?"

Now Ellen makes a face. "Do you have somewhere you'd rather be?"

A younger Jeff would not recognize that as a trap question. But this is not his first rodeo so he knows to tread lightly. "No, it's just that I told the guys I'd come meet them at the Cedar Room tonight."

"So you'd rather spend time with them than me?"

"I'd rather spend time with you AND with them before the day is through," Jeff says, hoping it would end this line of questioning.

It did not.

"I just don't understand. If we're going to make this work, we have to make a commitment to each other. That means putting each other first. We have to be the most important person in each others' lives, not friends or colleagues.

"I'm not talking about work associates. It's Niko and Louie."

"I just don't see why you need to spend all your time with friends when we're in a relationship."

Jeff has a choice. Soldier on and deal with the fallout or cut bait here and prevent the situation from escalating. He reaches for his phone and hits a number in his recently called list. He waits for a few moments and leaves a voicemail. "Hey Niko, I won't be able to make it out tonight. I have to help Ellen with some IKEA shopping and a couple of errands. I'll try to meet up with you guys soon."

***

Niko walks into the Cedar Room and as he approaches the table, sees that he has a missed call from Jeff. As he takes his seat, he listens to the voicemail. It's clear from his pained expression, he is not listening to good news. He hangs up and puts down his phone.

"He's not coming, is he?" Ashley asks, already knowing the answer. Jeff had no idea the whole purpose of getting the gang back together was to get Jeff and Ashley together in the same room.

Ashley was extremely reluctant to agree and now she feels like Jeff let her down yet again.

Niko is crestfallen. "I'm sorry, he has to go IKEA shopping with Ellen."

"Who's IKEA shopping?" Louie asks as he arrives just in time to catch the last part of the conversation.

"Jeff and Ellen," Niko says.

"Jeff hates IKEA," Louie says.

"How could anyone hate IKEA?" Ashley asks.

"It's a whole Ninja/Commando raid thing," Louie says as if that is supposed to clear everything up for her.

Niko slams his hand down on the table and leans forward. "Guys, it's happening and we need to stop it!"

Ashley looks perplexed. She looks at Niko then at Louie to see if he knows what Niko is talking about. "What is happening?"

"The six-month backslide," Niko says.

"What is that? Is that another one of your theories like the low hanging fruit?"

"It's not a theory. It's a natural law of the universe. When a couple has been together for more than three years, no break-up or separation is complete until they make it through the six-month backslide. Six months is just enough time to forget about why you broke up in the first place. You start to miss the good things about the other person and before you know it – it's already done. This is why most backslides happen at the six-month mark."

"And you think this is happening with Jeff and Ellen?"

"It's a classic six-month backslide. That's why you can't badmouth a friend's ex until they have safely made it through the backslide window. Let's call this the Louie/Horseface rule."

"I stand by what I said. She has a face like a horse."

"You called a woman horseface?" Ashley asks indignantly.

"Well, not to her unnaturally elongated face."

"Every time he saw Julie, he'd find a way to say, 'Aw Julie, why the long face'?" Niko added.

"Okay, maybe not my best moment," Louie says.

"So you admit you were a dick but you still stand behind it," Niko says. "Sounds like someone wants to eat their cake and have it too."

Now Louie springs to life. "Did I just catch the grammar police in a mistake? I think you meant to say 'have your cake and eat it too'."

"No, I said it the right way."

"That's not the way everyone else on the planet says it."

"I know and they're all wrong. That way doesn't make sense. If you give me a cake, I can have it and show it to everyone for three or four days. I can possess the cake and enjoy every second of it, and THEN I can eat it. Here's what I can't do – eat the cake and then have it to show everyone. I <u>can</u> have my cake and eat it too. I <u>can't</u> eat my cake and have it too."

"As much as I've missed the deep dives into the nuances of the English language, I feel like we've gotten off track," Ashley says. "We were talking about the backslide thingy."

Niko perks up. "Right. We need to save Jeff from himself. We have to stop the backslide. Ashley, how do we stop the backslide?"

"Wait, why am I in charge of this?"

"I thought you might have some expertise in relationships that we could exploit to our advantage."

"Oh, well when you put it like that..." Ashley says. "Here's what I can tell you. Every woman has a key 'influencer.' That one trusted source whose opinion they value, maybe even more than their own. The Gayle to their Oprah."

Niko and Louie stare at her blankly.

"The Robin to their Batman."

Suddenly they nod in comprehension. "I think I know who that is," Niko says. "She's always talking about her friend Caitlyn. I think Caitlyn is her influencer. Louie, you need to get in Caitlyn's ear and get her into Ellen's ear. Caitlyn has to convince Ellen getting back with Jeff is a terrible idea."

"What do we do about Jeff?" Louie asks.

"You leave that to me," Niko says confidently.

***

Jeff walks out of his bedroom holding up two similar blue button-down shirts. "Which one of these is more dinner-party chic?"

Niko doesn't even look up from his laptop. "Why would you ever need to know that?"

"I'm going to a dinner party with Ellen's co-workers and the dress code is dinner-party chic."

"Sounds like you just need to dress like a complete douchebag and you'll be fine."

"Thanks, that's...helpful?"

"Hey, here's a question for you. Have you spoken to Ashley lately?"

Jeff is a bit perplexed. Where is Niko going with this? "No, I haven't spoken to her since the cottage, actually."

"Why don't you meet her for a coffee?"

"Is there a specific reason why I should?"

"Don't you miss hanging out?"

Jeff ponders this for a few seconds. "I guess. I mean I always enjoy it when we get to spend time together."

"I'm just saying, meet her for a coffee. I think she could really use a friend right now."

***

Something is different this time. Sitting in a neighborhood coffee shop, Ashley is tending to her mint green tea while Jeff is getting the cream and sweetener mix in his coffee just right. There is a tension between them that they've never experienced before. They've always been very relaxed and natural around each other. The ability to be themselves in each other's company is a big part of why they always felt this close connection. As they struggle to find a conversation starter, both feel like they are in a strange new world.

"How have you been?" Jeff asks.

"I've been great thanks, and you?"

"Very good."

With this area of conversation exhausted, they sit in silence for another ten seconds which feels like ten hours. Ashley sits up in her chair and takes a formal tone. "Jeff, I've really enjoyed these last six months, but I feel like we're both in a different place in our lives right now. Do you know what I'm saying?"

A realization dawns on Jeff and he breaks out into a wide grin.

"What? What's so funny?" Ashley asks nervously.

"I've heard this conversation, this tone before. This is the Greg tone. Wait, are you breaking up with me?" Jeff asks jokingly. Ashley doesn't crack a smile. Now Jeff's smile quickly disappears. "Oh my God, you are breaking up with me. How is that possible? We're not even a couple!"

"I'm thinking it's time I went somewhere else for a while. This seems like the right time for a fresh start and I think I want to give myself that."

"Fresh start? To do what?"

"Everything's on the table. I always wanted to get my master's degree. I'm looking into different grad schools."

"You can't go," Jeff says.

"Why not, Jeff? What's keeping me here? Give me one good reason why I need to stay here!"

Jeff's cell phone rings. He picks it up but doesn't recognize the number. "I'm sorry. I need to see who this is."

Jeff gets up and steps outside to take the call. Ashley takes a sip of her tea as she tries to assess how she feels about what just happened. Her best guess is a mix of relief and sadness. The call didn't last long but it clearly had an impact on Jeff. As he sits back down, Ashley can tell he seems a bit shaken or out of sorts.

"Good Lord, you're white as a ghost. Who died?" she asks in an attempt at levity.

Jeff just looks up at her. "Dr. Moore."

Tony Sekulich

CHAPTER SEVENTEEN

The stillness of the lawyer's office waiting room gave Jeff an uneasy feeling. Although, one would be hard-pressed to think of a scenario where someone would be excited to be sitting in a lawyer's office. It's not like anyone ever burst into a room and said, "Hey kids, guess who gets to go to the lawyer's office?" followed by the euphoric cries of a bunch of seven-year-olds.

Granted, it's not as bad as sitting in a dentist's office or hospital waiting room, but there is still something unsettling about it. One thought strikes Jeff as he sees the diplomas hanging on the wall. Why is it the most educated amongst us seem to be the most insecure about proving how educated they are? Yes, we get it, you have multiple degrees. Your parents must be very proud.

"He's ready for you now, Mr. Dempsey."

The receptionist's voice interrupted what was building up to be a pretty good rant in Jeff's head. Oh well, he'll have to put a pin in it for another time. Jeff gets up and follows the receptionist into a large office where a middle-aged man in a dark blue suit gets up from behind his desk and offers his hand to Jeff.

"Nice to meet you, Jeff. I'm Leonard, you can call me Len. I'm Dr. Moore's attorney. I'm very sorry for your loss." Jeff shakes his hand.

"Thank you," he says with just a bit of hesitation. It feels weird taking ownership of 'the loss.' Len motions to Jeff to sit down and Jeff obliges.

"As I'm sure you're aware, Dr. Moore has named you executor of his estate."

As soon as he looked up and saw the shocked and horrified look on Jeff's face, it became clear that this was news to Jeff. Jeff's expression would not have changed an iota if the lawyer said, 'As I'm sure you're aware, a pack of rabid wolverines will be charging through that door to tear you limb from limb.'

"Excuse me?" is all Jeff could spit out at that particular moment.

"I'm sorry, I thought you knew. Stephen, er, I mean Dr. Moore didn't have any close living family. He has some distant nieces and nephews, but they were family by blood only. They barely saw him in his later years. He always said you were the only family he had."

Jeff is overwhelmed to hear this, but he really shouldn't be. When Jeff was a student at Holy Trinity, he had Dr. Moore as a teacher for two years of chemistry. They had a very good teacher-student relationship. Dr. Moore would always ask him about his basketball exploits. He never went to any of the games because he felt it was beneath him. But he genuinely cared about how Jeff was doing and, for his part, Jeff could sense there was something special about this teacher.

Jeff's favorite story was the time he came to class late because of a dentist appointment and when he walked into the classroom, every pair of eyes followed him from the door to his desk. Occasionally, they would look over at Dr. Moore and then back to Jeff. It was creepy and bizarre and Jeff couldn't imagine why he was such a spectacle.

After the class, Dr. Moore waved him up to the front of the class and explained what he missed. After too many students were stragglers coming in and getting ready to start on time, Dr. Moore threw one of his hall-of-fame temper tantrums. He screamed and broke his yardstick over a student's desk. He lectured them about punctuality and how the lack of it was a sign of disrespect. He vowed that the next person to walk through his door late for class would feel the wrath of Almighty God come down upon him.

"Why didn't you freak out on me then?" Jeff asked.

"I figured you had a good excuse. And besides, I had already accomplished what I needed to. Students will take advantage of my kindness and gentleness, so every once in a while, I need to put on a fireworks display to snap them back in line."

While the rest of the class rushed to Chemistry class in fear for the rest of that semester, Jeff got a glimpse of the man behind the curtain. It meant a lot that Dr. Moore shared that with him.

Jeff lost touch with him through his 20's, but at the ten-year reunion, they reconnected and started going for coffee once a week. The weekly 'coffee break' was something that Jeff wrote in ink in his calendar. It was never to be missed. And it never was.

About six years ago, Dr. Moore was suffering from dementia and had to move into an assisted living facility. Jeff would come by and make him dinner at least one day a week. On another day in the week, he would take Dr. Moore out to dinner at Clive's, his favorite steakhouse.

Dessert at Clive's was the highlight of Jeff's week. Not because the ice cream was the best he'd ever had, but rather because of the dance that would ensue immediately after they finished their main course.

"How about some ice cream, Dr. Moore?"

The elderly man would start to wave his hands and shake his head. "No, no, I couldn't."

If you scoured the planet, you might find five people who love ice cream more than this man. But he grew up at the tail end of the Great Depression and he developed a reflex to say no to seconds or dessert. Those were luxuries that his family could not afford and so he viewed giving in to the urges as almost sinful.

So Jeff would order a dish of ice cream and when it came, he just set it on the table and watched Dr. Moore react. Imagine you were sitting across from a trained circus tiger and you just slammed down a piece of raw beef. The tiger would resist pouncing on it, but it would not be able to hide its mouth-watering desire.

This was how Dr. Moore was with the ice cream. His eyes never left it. You could see he wanted it so badly. Jeff would pretend like he wouldn't see this and just let the ice cream begin to melt. Finally...

"Whose ice cream is that?" Dr. Moore would inquire as casually as he could.

"Oh, that's mine."

"Oh, okay," he would say with great disappointment.

"I don't think I can eat all of it. Do you think you might be able to help me out?"

"I might be able to have a spoonful."

"Okay then, let's dig in," Jeff would say as they each grabbed a spoon.

If Jeff got two spoonfuls of that ice cream, it was a good day. Dr. Moore tore into that ice cream like a death row inmate devouring his last dessert.

"Will you do it?"

The lawyer's voice snapped Jeff out of his fond ice cream memory.

"Do what?"

"Fulfill the duties of the executor."

"I have a choice?"

"You can petition to be removed as executor. But if I'm being honest, I don't know who else would do it."

"Can I take a few days to think it over," Jeff asks.

"Of course. However, there is one matter that is more pressing."

"Do I want to know?"

"Dr. Moore has asked that you give the eulogy at his funeral mass."

***

"You understand what you have to do, right?" Niko is in full teacher mode. As a rule, he doesn't like to speak to his friends in the same manner he addresses his fourth-graders when he is pressing upon them extremely important instructions. But desperate times call for desperate measures and Niko blew well past desperate about two weeks ago.

"Yes, I got it. I'm not an idiot," Louie protests.

"All evidence to the contrary," Niko mutters under his breath. "Okay then, walk me through it."

"I reach out to Caitlyn, find a reason to get together for drinks and start talking about Jeff and Ellen."

"Don't make..."

Louie cuts him off. "Don't make it too obvious what we're trying to do. Be subtle, be smooth. I can do it."

"Sorry Lou, but subtle and smooth aren't your strong suits."

"Hey, I can be subtle and smooth when I want to."

"Like at Ellen's 30th birthday party?"

"How long am I going to have to hear about that?"

"Until I'm dead or lobotomized."

***

In May 2007, Jeff threw a huge house party for Ellen's 30th birthday. He invited a large group consisting of both her friends and his. Her most favorite gift was a ceramic vase brought in from China. She always desired the finer things in life and she felt a Chinese handcrafted vase would look great in their front foyer.

Louie had just gone through a bad break-up and decided that he would blow off some steam. Forgoing the fancy appetizers, he decided to stick to a brown bottle diet.

"I've had six beers," he would proudly declare to the room.

"I've had nine beers!"

"I've had 13 beers!"

When the inevitable alcohol-induced vomiting came knocking on his door, Louie didn't panic. He knew he had time to make it to the downstairs bathroom. However, when he found that occupied, genuine panic started to settle in.

He bolted for the front door hoping to make it outside. This turned out to be too ambitious. When he started puking he was still inside the front door and the only receptacle in sight was...Ellen's brand new Chinese vase.

A little while later Jeff could see that Ellen was furious about something but didn't know what. "What's up with Ellen?" Jeff asked Niko who was passing by.

"Oh yeah, she's pissed off right now."

"Why is she pissed off?"

"It was something Louie said."

"What did Louie say?"

"Bleeeccchhhh!" Niko says doing his best puking imitation.

***

A thought has just occurred to Louie. "Oh God, Caitlin was there that night. Do you think she remembers?"

"No, I'm sure she's forgotten all about it," Niko offers in a reassuring manner.

"Really?"

"Don't be a moron. Not a chance."

"It doesn't matter. I'm fairly certain I know what to do."

"I know you are," Niko says. "That's what terrifies me."

***

Jeff paces around Ashley's apartment. He's talking out loud but it's not clear he's actually engaging her in conversation.

"I can't do it. I really don't think I can do it," he says aloud but to no one in particular.

For her part, walking Jeff back from the ledge is becoming old hat now. "Take a breath; let's deal with it piece by piece. What specifically do you feel you can't handle?"

"Do you know what being an executor entails?"

"Not really."

"It's not just going through their stuff and allocating what he wants to give away in the will. It's a never-ending responsibility. There's dealing with the bank, the cable company, the credit card company, the estate's taxes. Imagine the most boring, awful minutiae of your daily life and then double it. That's what's just happened to me."

"Okay, those are all the reasons not to do it. What are the reasons to do it?"

"There's only one. It's Dr. Moore."

"There you go. It looks like the pros outweigh the cons. You could never turn your back on him."

"But the eulogy. I can't get up in front of all those people and talk about his life."

Ashley walks right up and looks deep into his eyes. "Listen to me, Jeff. You CAN do this. You will find a way."

"You really think so?"

"Trust me. I'd never steer you wrong, Jeff."

Something weird was happening ever since I found out about Dr. Moore's death. It's like memories that had been buried deep in my psyche for decades were suddenly playing out in front of me like a scene from a movie. I don't know what these memories mean. I just know I can't stop them when they come.

March 1995

In a flash, Jeff is transported back to the Holy Trinity main hallway the Monday after his 51-point game against Franklin Heights in the Provincial Semi-Finals. If he feels like he's the big man on campus, it's probably because he can't walk ten feet without someone giving him a high-five or slapping him on the back.

But there was one person in particular who hung in the background and just watched. When Jeff saw Ginny standing alone by her locker, he made a point to go up to her.

She couldn't hide her smile when she saw him approach. "Didn't I tell you you'd have a big game?"

"I guess I owe you a huge thank you."

"No thanks necessary."

"It's weird, I had no idea I was flaring my elbow out when I took a jump shot."

"You'd have no reason to. It's the way you always shoot," Ginny says matter-of-factly.

"Wait, what?!?"

"You always shoot with your elbow out. Your elbow wasn't the problem. I could see you were too much in your own head and you were beating yourself up over it."

"So what you said was all bullshit?"

"Basically. But it got you out of your head. And once you thought you had it fixed, your confidence came flooding back."

Jeff doesn't know what to do with this information. She clearly was screwing with his head but to amazing results. "I don't know whether or not I should listen to anything else you say," he says.

"Oh, you definitely should. I'd never steer you wrong, Jeff."

∗∗

Sitting at his regular table in the Cedar Room, Louie feels a bit like he is in Bizarro World. Usually, he's nervous because he has to find a way to convince a woman to overlook his obvious flaws and go out with him anyway. Tonight, he has to convince a woman to try to convince a friend to dump someone.

"Is this ironic?" he says out loud.

"Is what ironic?" Caitlyn says as she arrives at the table.

Now Louie's flustered for a whole different reason. "No, I was just singing to myself. I just can't get enough Alanis, but then again who can, right?"

She gives him an odd look as she sits down. It's a look Louie has seen many times before.

"Anyway, it's nice to meet you," Louie says trying to keep the conversation moving.

"Are we meeting for the first time?" Caitlyn asks. "I feel like we may have met before."

"Oh, I don't think so. I would have definitely remembered that. But you know what, I get that a lot. People always come up to me and say, 'Hey, aren't you the guy who did that really stupid embarrassing thing?' And I have to say nope, it must have been someone who looks just like me."

"Okay. What's on your mind?"

"You're a friend of Ellen's. I'm a friend of Jeff's. I thought we should have a drink."

"Sure, why not?"

Karlie comes by to take their drink order. Louie orders a beer while Caitlyn orders a Malbec. Louie decides the only option is to jump right into it.

"How about that Jeff and Ellen situation? Is that not the craziest thing?"

"They must know what they're doing. It must be fate bringing them back together."

"Is it though? I mean, it didn't end well for either of them the first time. I'd sure hate to see them go through that again. And as the friends, we're the ones left picking up the pieces. Am I right?"

Karlie comes back with the drinks, saving Caitlyn from having to answer that question. Caitlyn raises her glass in a toast. "Here's to the heart getting what it wants."

Louie raises his glass and clinks hers. She holds eye contact for an unusually long time.

"Can I ask you something, Louie?"

"Sure."

"Does your wife or girlfriend feel the same way about this as you?"

Louie almost falls out of his chair. He is in Bizarro World. Every other time, he's the one who gets 'boyfriended.' That's when a woman is afraid you're going to ask her out and drops a pre-emptive boyfriend mention. But he's never had anyone do the significant other fishing expedition. He tries to remain cool.

"Actually, I am currently single."

"Oh really," she says with great interest as she takes a drink of her wine. "You're right, it would really suck if they were to split up again."

Louie feels like he's made huge progress. "It really would."

"Because that would mean that we wouldn't get to spend time together."

"What's that now?"

"I think it would be really great if the four of us went out to dinner sometime. Maybe even dancing afterward. Does that sound like fun to you?"

Niko could not have been clearer about the mission objective. So Louie can't plead ignorance for what he's about to say next.

"I'd love that."

"I mean, I can't think of a good reason why we shouldn't do that this weekend. Can you?"

This is a character-defining moment for Louie. Take one for the team and stick to the mission, or chuck it all away for his own personal benefit. Which way will he go?

"No, no I cannot."

Was there ever any doubt?

***

The morning of Dr. Moore's wake, Jeff is at Ellen's getting dressed and ready to go. As he tightens his tie, he is still waffling about accepting the duties of executor. "I would never want to say no to his wishes, but I feel like it's asking a lot of me. Maybe too much."

"Oh for God's sake, just blow it off then," Ellen says as she enters the bedroom.

"You really think I should?"

"It sounds like a major pain in the ass and he didn't even ask you first."

"He did have dementia, maybe he thought he had."

"We haven't even seen the will yet. Do you even know what he left us?" She quickly catches herself. "You. What he left you."

Jeff is a bit taken aback by what he just heard. "No, I have no idea and it doesn't matter. This isn't a quid pro quo situation. There will be a formal reading of the will next week and that will all come to light then."

Ellen puts the finishing touches on her makeup but says nothing. It's almost as if she's already checked out of the conversation.

"Just to be clear," Jeff says. "Your advice is I should not do it?"

She quickly spins on her heel. "Look, do it. Don't do it. I don't give a shit. I'm just saying you're getting all worked up and for what?"

Jeff doesn't respond but just thinks about what she just said.

***

Jeff is one of the first to arrive at the wake. An elderly lady recognizes Jeff from his frequent visits to the assisted living facility and comes over and takes hold of Jeff's hand. "Oh dear, I am so sorry for your loss."

"I appreciate that. It's mostly your fault," Jeff says solemnly.

Okay, I know what you're thinking. That's a serious dick move. And you're not wrong, but you have to understand one thing – I had no option! Dr. Moore left a very detailed list of instructions for the wake and funeral. I'll get to them all in due time, but first on that list is: If anyone expresses their condolences by saying "I'm so sorry," I am to tell them, "I appreciate that, it's mostly your fault."

I had no idea his burial services would come with such a wacky list of rules. Although really, I should have seen it coming.

June 2012

Jeff walks into Dr. Moore's room in the assisted living facility carrying a glass of water. He sets it down beside his bed. "One glass of cold water. Anything else I can get you?"

"Kid, listen to what I'm telling you. My funeral is going to be unlike anything you've ever seen."

"Please, I won't be around for it. You'll outlive me by a good 15 years."

"You just watch. It's not going to be all this gloom and doom. I don't want that. I want mine to be an event where people say, 'That was the most fun I've ever had at a funeral'."

"You want people to have fun at your funeral?"

"Absolutely! I'm talking balloons for the kids, a petting zoo outside, the whole shebang."

"That's not the way it usually works," Jeff says.

"I know the way it usually works. That's why I want to do something different. Most people see the word funeral and they go right to sadness. I look at the word funeral and all I see is an anagram for R-E-A-L F-U-N"

He was right. That's what I loved about the man. He was able to make you see things in a different light. I loved him for that. But as the day went on, the sheer volume of people and the enormity of the responsibility started to weigh on me.

Later in the day, Louie arrives at the wake with his date, Caitlyn. When Niko sees this, only the societal convention of not screaming and flipping tables during a wake kept him from completely exploding right there on the spot. Still, he marches over and pulls Louie by the arm into one of the private rooms nearby.

"What is she doing here? Is she your date?"

"Of course not? She's my...escort"

"I'd rather you'd brought an actual hooker."

"I know it looks bad but it's like in *The Art of War* – Keep your friends close and your enemies closer."

"No, it's like in *Backstabbing Louie Tries To Get Laid* – Screw over your friends if it means getting some."

Ashley comes tearing into the room. "Hey, idiots. Everyone can hear you. Where's Jeff? I haven't seen him for ages."

I don't know I haven't seen him fo-" Niko stops in mid-sentence as he looks at his phone. "Uh-oh!"

"What Uh-oh?" Ashley says.

Niko reads a text message from Jeff. "Really sorry guys but I can't do the executor thing and I can't do the eulogy tomorrow. I'll see you in a few days."

The three look at each other in silence.

Tony Sekulich

CHAPTER EIGHTEEN

The Cedar Room has always been a sanctuary for the gang. It's the place where they go to seek refuge from the choppy waters and dark skies of everyday life. And so in a time where weird has become the new normal, the feeling they have sitting at their usual table is one of general uneasiness.

Just as Ashley's absence cast a pall over Sunday brunch, Jeff's empty chair at the table makes it seemingly impossible for Niko, Louie, and Ashley to relax. Dr. Moore's wake ended only a few hours ago and his funeral will take place in about 12 hours from now. And since we're counting hours, it's been more than seven since the last time any of them had a confirmed Jeff Dempsey sighting.

Niko and Louie have known Jeff for an eternity, but they can't come up with a good lead on where he could be. He's not at Ellen's, his parent's place, his sister's place, their favorite wing place, or Jeff's favorite dumplings place.

Just to be extra thorough, Louie made sure Jeff wasn't at any of the strip clubs in the city. Good ole' Louie, always selflessly going the extra mile for a friend.

"I'm out of ideas, I have no sweet clue where he could be," Niko announces as he brings a fresh round of drinks to the table. Louie and Ashley gladly grab a much-needed drink after a long day that shows no sign of letting up anytime soon.

Louie turns to Ashley. "Aren't you supposed to be some kind of psychic/voodoo person? Shouldn't you be able to find him?"

"What is it that you think I do, exactly?" Ashley asks.

For his part, Niko can't stop thinking about the logistical ramifications of the situation. "What do we do if he doesn't show up to deliver that eulogy? We can't leave Dr. Moore hanging like that."

"I'll do it," Louie says matter-of-factly.

"NO!!!!" both Niko and Ashley cry out in unison.

Before Louie can make his case as to why he would be the perfect replacement, a fourth shows up to join them at the table.

"Caitlyn, you made it!" Louie says.

She comes over and gives Louie a quick embrace and sits down in what should be Jeff's seat. There's not one bit of this that is sitting well with Niko.

"Caitlyn's here," Niko says through gritted teeth. "Why is Caitlyn here? Why are you here?" he says turning towards her.

Ashley ignores Niko's rudeness and poses a friendlier question to Caitlyn. "Have you heard anything from Ellen? Does she know where Jeff is right now?"

Caitlyn looks sullen. "No, she hasn't heard anything. I hope he's okay."

"You're not here with news about Jeff?" Niko says.

"No, I'm here to spend some time with Louie."

"REALLY???" Once again, Niko and Ashley respond perfectly in sync.

"This Louie?" Niko says pointing to Louie like a witness identifying the murderer in a courtroom.

"You bet! Isn't he something?"

"Oh, he's something all right," Niko says. "Modern science just can't quite determine what."

"Well, I think he's a real cutie."

"SERIOUSLY???" Yet again, Niko and Ashley respond as one.

"Okay, we need to stop doing that," Ashley says.

Niko cannot stop thinking about their predicament. "Guys we need to figure out where he is soon or this is going to be a disaster. There's got to be a place we're missing."

March 1995

It's been three days since the Holy Trinity High School boys' basketball team won the 1995 Provincial Championship. Ginny has arrived at the school gym a full hour and a half before classes start and a good hour before the first students will be arriving.

She prefers to do her equipment manager duties early so she can get her work done undisturbed. Her task for that morning is to input the stats from the provincial playoffs into the brand new computer system in the Athletic Director's office, just off the main gym.

This is her first experience working with Windows '95 and she's fairly certain this is the most advanced computing platform she will ever use. Hey, cut her some slack, it was 1995.

This thought is interrupted by a familiar sound coming from the gym. It's the sound of a basketball bouncing off the hardwood and occasionally 'swishing' the mesh.

Ginny wanders out to see Jeff in his street clothes, shooting baskets in the empty gym.

"Have you come down from the high yet?" she asks.

Jeff doesn't look at her as he fires up another shot. "Nope, not yet."

"You guys played great. You played great."

"Thanks."

After a few seconds of awkward silence, Ginny starts to head back to her computer work. She only takes a few steps when…

"Hey, you doing anything Friday night?"

This freezes her in her tracks. Did he just ask what she thinks he asked?

"This Friday?"

"Yeah, the guys are throwing a Purple Jesus party to celebrate the Provincial title. It's going to be epic. You should come."

"Thanks, but that's not really my scene. And my Mom would never allow it."

"Your call. But you really did help the other day. I can promise you, I'll never forget it."

"I'm glad." There is another prolonged silence for a few moments. "Do you usually hang out in the gym by yourself?"

"I like to come here when nobody else is here and shoot around some. It's not for practice. It's where I can do my best thinking."

"Makes sense."

"So, I guess I'll see you around then," he says casually.

"We don't really run in the same circles."

"Then...until we meet again."

Ginny smiles. "Until we meet again."

***

Ashley awakens and sits upright in her bed. She's trying to make sense of what she just experienced. She was just in the gym with Jeff right after they won Provincials.

Was it a dream? It couldn't be because it actually happened. She remembers every bit of it. So what do you call it when you dream of something that actually happened? Is her subconscious trying to send her a message? If so, what?

Then it dawns on her. There was only one pertinent piece of information that could be of any use. It seemed like a lottery shot but it's the only hunch she's had since Jeff disappeared.

Just under an hour later, Ashley arrives at Holy Trinity School and heads straight downstairs to the gym. While she has no business being there, she is moving with such focus and determination, nobody thinks to stop and question her. It is true that if you act like you are supposed to be somewhere, people will generally assume you belong. This plays to her advantage this morning but is still a bit unsettling that apparently anyone can just waltz into a high school unchecked.

When she hears that familiar sound once again, she says a quiet thank you to her guardian angels who pointed her in the right direction. Even though logically it is 100 times more likely to be a student in the gym, she knows in her gut, it's Jeff.

And she's right.

"You're still flaring out your elbow," she says with a smile.

"Did you come here to drag me to the funeral?" he asks with just a hint of accusation.

"I came to make sure you're okay." She looks around like she's expecting someone to come barging in at any moment. "How are we not getting thrown out of here?"

"I told the Athletic Director I'm an alumnus who's getting ready to deliver Dr. Moore's eulogy."

"Are you?"

"If I can get into the headspace. It's why I came here."

"Does giving that eulogy really have you twisted up this badly?"

"It's not the eulogy...well, not just that. This may not make sense, but I can't shake the feeling that I have this huge life choice to make and the window to make it is closing quickly. The thing is, I'm not even sure what the decision is."

"Believe it or not, I know how you feel. Let's just tackle this one step at a time. About the eulogy, don't think of it as a burden."

"How else can I think of it?"

"Do you know how many lives he touched over the years? And of all those people, he asked you to pay tribute to his life and his career. It really is a tremendous honor."

"I just wish I could make myself see it that way."

"Here's what I'm going to do. Sometimes when my clients are stuck on one particular issue, I'll write them out a key."

"A key?"

"It's a phrase or sentence that helps them gain perspective in the moment and hopefully, enables them to move forward. Even if it's just a step or two."

Ashley pulls out a notepad and a pen from her purse and begins to write something. She folds the piece of paper and hands it to Jeff. "When you get up there and you feel like you can't go forward, look at this and it will get you through."

***

As Jeff steps foot inside St. Malachy's Catholic Church, he freezes. Ashley continues ahead, not yet noticing that Jeff is immobile just inside the doorway. He is immediately struck by a sense of déjà vu. There is something familiar about this situation.

And then it hits him.

Just like the first night he "re-met" Ashley, she had to talk him into giving a speech he was more than a little reluctant to give. The thought makes him smile but isn't enough to snap him out of his temporary paralysis.

From behind an elderly gentleman places his hand on Jeff's shoulder. "He was a good man. I'm very sorry."

"I appreciate that. It's mostly your fault."

With that, Jeff bounds forward and takes his seat in a reserved section of the pews.

Here's the thing you have to know about the Catholic Funeral Mass. It's one of the only services that has the choose-your-own-adventure feature. The family has the option of going with the full Mass with all the bells and whistles or an abbreviated version. There is also the opportunity to add personal touches to pay tribute to important aspects of the deceased's life. In this case, one of Dr. Moore's greatest passions were bagpipes. As such, it was very important to him that this be included in the service.

A bagpiper in full Highland dress stands at the front of the church and plays a solemn and hauntingly beautiful rendition of Amazing Grace. The funeral attendees are captivated by the blissful melodies that fill the room. Needless to say, they are more than a little shocked when four men in the front jump up, grab the bagpiper, throw him to the ground and start punching and kicking him.

Oh yeah, one thing I forgot to mention...Dr. Moore HATED bagpipes. Would you expect anything less from the guy who turns "funeral" into "real fun?" And the bagpiper, while initially frightened, wasn't hurt. They were pulling their punches and kicks. It was more of a symbolic beat-down. It's just a shame Dr. Moore couldn't be there to see it. Anyway, after they tossed him out the side door, the funeral could continue with its regularly scheduled programming. And next on the agenda was...the eulogy.

Jeff steps up to the pulpit and pulls a piece of paper out of his pocket. He scribbled down a few thoughts to carry him through. He didn't want to write out a full text for fear of it sounding too rigid. Or that's what he told himself. If he were being totally honest, he'd tell you he couldn't bring himself to commit those thoughts to writing.

"What can you say about a man...." He catches himself. That's a terrible beginning. He looks for a better opening. "When God made Dr. Moore he..." Oh come on, that's even worse, he thinks to himself.

Two false starts and now panic is beginning to set in. "Webster's dictionary defines greatness as..." Are you kidding me! That's the worst! Jeff's inner critic is throwing a hissy fit and it doesn't look like he's going to get through this.

Then he catches Ashley's glance. She gives him a subtle nod. Jeff exhales and reaches in his shirt pocket. He pulls out the key and opens it up. It reads...

You don't <u>have to</u> give the eulogy. You <u>get to</u> give the eulogy.

Upon reading it, Jeff is rocked on his feet. What is this power she has to reach through his inner turmoil and get to the heart of it? In an instant, he is taken back to...

July 2005

Jeff and Dr. Moore sit outside on a sidewalk patio enjoying a cold beer as they wrap up a game of chess. After reconnecting at the 10 year-reunion the previous month, they made a point to get together on a regular basis. These meet-ups became known as 'coffee breaks' despite the fact very little coffee was consumed.

Once Dr. Moore cornered Jeff's queen, the match was over. Jeff hauls out his flip phone and looks at the time. "I've got to run. I have to go meet my friends for drinks."

Dr. Moore suddenly turns very serious. "Jeff my boy, don't ever let me catch you saying that again."

Jeff is taken aback. Dr. Moore had a naturally jovial disposition, so the serious tone is a bit surprising and unsettling for Jeff. He can't even respond.

"There is nothing more precious than the opportunity to spend time with the people you really care about. There are so many people in this world who will pull you down and try to make you feel less than. When you have a chance to spend time with those who make you feel special and appreciated, cherish it," Dr. Moore says.

"But how do I know who belongs in each category?"

"Remember what I taught you about litmus tests? They will always give you the answer?"

"That's great advice, but how do I do that in everyday life?"

"Ask yourself this question – do I have to spend time with this person, or do I get to spend time with this person?" Jeff smiles broadly as he takes this in. "So you were saying?" Dr. Moore adds.

"I have to run. I <u>get to</u> spend time with my friends."

THE NEW TWENTY

***

In real time, Jeff paused for no more than a couple of seconds but in his head, he re-lived the entire incident. And when he snapped back to reality, everything suddenly started to come into sharp focus for him. He crumpled up the paper with his scribbled notes and adopted a more relaxed stance.

"You know what the problem with eulogies is? You're always too late in saying what you need to say to someone. There are so many things I could tell you about Dr. Moore. What he meant to me and so many other people."

Jeff is lost in a thought and starts chuckling.

"He was the funniest person I knew. Those who knew him only as a scholar and teacher may not have appreciated it, but he made me laugh every time we were together. And making him laugh was the highlight of my day. With the notable exception of the bagpiper, I think you all appreciated his sense of humor today."

The gathered crowd breaks out into laughter.

"I could go on but what's the point? It's all stuff I should have said two weeks ago, two months ago, two years ago."

Again, he catches Ashley's glance and looks deep into her eyes. "Wouldn't it be great if just once you could tell that person what they need to hear before it's too late?"

There's a flash of something in Ashley's eyes. Where is he going with this?

"A very wise person once told me that to become the best version of myself, I had to do one thing every day that the old me was too afraid to do."

One of the mourners turns to the person beside her. "He was a very wise man indeed," she whispers.

"I thought I knew what that meant but I don't think I fully realized the significance until right now. You see, I almost wasn't here today. I almost fell back into being the old Jeff Dempsey who was governed by fear and small thinking. But someone helped me see that this is no way to go through life. I was lost in the wilderness and they found me, shone a light and said follow me, I'll never steer you wrong."

Jeff is hit with a series of quick-hit flashbacks.

In school after the 51-point game.... "I don't know whether or not I should listen to anything else you say." "Oh, you definitely should. I'd never steer you wrong, Jeff."

At Ashley's apartment... "Trust me. I'd never steer you wrong, Jeff."

After a barely noticeable pause, Jeff soldiers on. He's picking up steam as he goes. "There really are two types of people in this world. Those who make you feel less than and those who convince you that you can be more than you ever dreamed."

Jeff catches himself in thought. He inhales deeply.

"The ones who love us best are the ones we'll lay to rest, and visit their graves on holidays at best. The ones who love us least are the ones we'll die to please. If it's any consolation I don't begin to understand it. I didn't write that. Paul Westerberg did but it seems to make more sense to me than ever before."

Jeff pauses as he momentarily scans the room.

"If you're wondering if someone falls into the category of the first kind or the second kind, here's a simple litmus test. The first kind are the people you *have to* spend time with. The second are the people, if you're lucky enough, you *get to* spend time with.

Now the flashbacks are hitting him like lightning bolts.

"Hey Niko, I won't be able to make it out tonight. I have to help Ellen with some IKEA shopping..."

Talking about Ashley with Niko... "I guess. I mean I always enjoy it when we get to spend time together."

Now he makes eye contact with Ellen.

"I spent way too much time trying to please someone who couldn't be pleased. Trying to fill that bottomless void left me shattered and almost unrecognizable from who I used to be."

And then I met one of the other types of people. The ones who fill you up rather than spiritually sucking you dry. They convince you that you can do almost anything. They believe in you even when you don't believe in yourself."

He chuckles to himself.

"And let me tell you, when you finally see it, you feel so stupid. How could you not have seen it all along? It was right in front of you and yet at the same time, invisible. Just like Dorothy's ruby slippers."

This inside baseball reference is lost on everyone except Ashley who can't fight off a little smile.

"All that time, they were there for you and you never really appreciated it. But then one day, it just hits you. That person, who you saw as a friend and a mentor, turns out to be so much more than that."

Jeff has now locked eyes with Ashley and holds her gaze.

"You realize – I am madly, deeply, completely in love with this person."

Ashley's jaw drops. The mourners who clearly thought he was talking about Dr. Moore now appear confused and more than a little uncomfortable. Ashley gets up and quickly leaves. Jeff sees her start to leave and looks for a way to wrap it up as quickly as he can.

"Dr. Moore was a great man who helped me as much in death as he did in life. I will carry his wisdom with me until the day I die. For that, I will be forever grateful."

Jeff rushes from the pulpit and starts for the main exit. He passes Ellen who is seated in the aisle towards the back of the church.

"What was that all about?" she hisses.

Jeff doesn't break stride. "Yeah, we're done. Have a nice life."

**

That may have been the first time Jeff ended a relationship while in a full sprint, but he wasn't thinking about that at the moment. He didn't know where Ashley was headed or even if he'd see her again. He just knew he couldn't let her go without saying what he needs to say.

Jeff stops in the middle of the public park and looks around in all directions. There, off to left, is Ashley in a full brisk walk. Jeff resumes his sprint and starts calling after her. "Ashley! Ashley!"

He catches up to her but is barely able to speak. He hasn't had to run like that since his ill-fated basketball comeback.

"It's you." He spits out between deep gasps of breath. "I was talking about you."

"Yeah, I got that."

"Then why are you running away?"

Ashley just shakes her head and searches for a way to explain what is going on inside of her.

"From the time I was 15-years-old, I dreamt of the day Jeff Dempsey would tell me he loved me. And now, that you have... "

"You're disappointed?" Jeff asks sheepishly.

"No, I'm terrified."

From Jeff's reaction, it's clear that's not the answer he was expecting.

"Do you know why they tell people recovering from addiction not to make any major life decisions for 12 months after recovery?"

Jeff shakes his head.

"It's because the brain needs to regain its chemical balance and, until it does, judgment can be seriously impaired during this process. Behavior can be manic and outlandish ideas can seem completely rational."

Jeff nods as she continues but still isn't sure what this has to do with him.

"The same thing happens when we're grieving. So as much as I want this to be real, I am petrified this is just grief brain acting out. And two months from now, you're going to look at me and no longer see this amazing woman you're completely in love with. You'll just see me as some chick you're banging."

Jeff takes her by both hands and steps just a little closer.

"I'll want you to be the only chick I'm banging two months from now, two years from now, two lifetimes from now."

Tears start to stream down Ashley's face. Jeff is convinced he's brought on tears of joy. He's not exactly on the mark.

"You want to know what's sad and pathetic? THAT is the most romantic thing anyone's ever said to me," Ashley says.

"Ashley, who knows what will happen in the future? I can't guarantee a perfect ending. Nobody can. What I do know is six months ago, I would not have been able to be standing here, looking you in the eyes and telling you that I love you. I'm only here, we're only here, because of you. Because you reached out and helped a broken man become whole again. But I won't be completely whole if you're not with me. So let's do that thing we're both afraid to do…together."

She searches for the appropriate response but can't find the words. Instead, she breaks out into a smile that tells Jeff all he needs to know. They look deep into each other's eyes then simultaneously lean in for the kiss of a lifetime.

***

After spending most of the remaining daylight hours back at Ashley's place for what we'll politely call 'grown-up alone time,' they figure they should meet up with Niko and Louie to break the news.

Jeff arrives at the table with a round of drinks for the gang minus Louie who is nowhere to be found. He sits down beside Ashley and puts his arm around the back of her chair. They smile at each other and then steal a quick kiss.

"Whoa, whoa, whoa," Niko says. "I'm as happy about this as anyone, but you gotta let me ease into it. It is still a little weird."

"Good weird, though?" Jeff asks.

"Very good weird," Ashley says which then leads to another kiss.

"Speaking of weird, where's Lou?" Niko asks.

"Getting his heart ripped out," Louie says arriving on the scene. He sits down and grabs Niko's beer and starts drinking it. "I'm telling you I am through with love. It's a mirage, it doesn't exist and I want nothing to do with it."

He looks up and sees Jeff and Ashley canoodling.

"Oh, come on! Seriously!"

"What happened with Caitlyn?" Ashley asks.

"Everything was great until big mouth here had to make his big speech," he says gesturing to Jeff.

Louie picks up the story right at the point when Jeff tells Ellen that it's over. Caitlyn and Louie are seated in the pews just behind Ellen, holding hands. After Jeff blows by them, dumping Ellen in the process, Caitlyn releases Louie's hand like she just found out it's radioactive.

"Oh, thank God!" she says. "Louie, we can't see each other anymore."

"Why not?"

"I'd rather not say."

"I believe I'm owed an explanation."

"Okay, well...have you ever heard of the six-month backslide?"

"I am familiar with it."

"Well, the rest of Ellen's friends saw that she and Jeff were falling into it, so we came up with a plan to try to break them up."

"Okay," Louie says tentatively.

"The plan was that if Ellen thought staying with Jeff would mean spending more time with you, she might break it off. No offense."

"Why do people keep saying that?"

***

"Wait, wait, wait," Niko blurts out, barely able to contain his glee. "While you bailed on our six-month backslide plan to pursue Caitlyn..."

"I was the key part of hers...and yes, I get that it's ironic."

Niko is simply beaming now. "I don't think I've ever been happier than I am right now."

Jeff looks at Ashley. "Me too!"

***

Jeff is seated in front of his computer wrapping up another of his New Twenty vlog posts.

So I know what you're thinking. Now that Ashley and I are a couple, is this the end of The New Twenty?

Ashley comes into the room and appears on screen holding up a flowery hand towel. "Jeff, you used the good towels again."

"Well, why do you put decorative towels in the bathroom in the first place? I wash my hands, I see a towel, I use it."

"Because it makes your disgusting boys bathroom just that much prettier."

"You want to pretty up the place? Put flowers in there. That way I won't be tempted to dry my hands on them."

Ashley leans in close and wraps her arms around him from behind. She gives him a kiss on the cheek. "If only I could believe that were true."

Jeff can't fight off a smile as she leaves the room.

"Are there some adjustments to make and questions still to be answered? Absolutely. But those questions can only be answered in time. So all I can tell you is..."

Ashley pops her head back in the room. "Are you almost ready to get going? The bold new adventures don't stop now that you have a girlfriend."

"*Stay tuned.*"

AUTHOR'S NOTES

If you're reading this, then you've likely bought and read the entirety of *The New Twenty*. And if that's the case, you will never know how grateful I am for that. But I'll try to explain it here.

By all rights, this book should never have come to be. In trying to get it made as a TV series, it faced more rejection than the chess club during prom season. But all the while, I believed in it and I thought these characters and their stories would resonate with an audience.

So when I discovered Wattpad, I saw an opportunity to reach an audience directly and see if I was right or if the gatekeepers were justified in turning it down. The results were beyond what I could have expected.

The degree to which this can be considered a success is due in large part to the loyal readers and fans of the book. After posting the first three stories, the readers' comments, votes, and messages are what fueled me to write the final three.

People have asked if it is autobiographical or completely made up. The answer is both. There is no character who is 100% based on any real person. I can be found in Jeff (found myself looking for a way to reinvent myself at 40) Niko (I HATE it when people misuse literally and ironically) and Louie (The 13 beer anecdote in the last story sadly saw me playing the Louie role in real life)

But there are little nods to real life people in here. I did play high school (JV) basketball with my good friend Junior. We did do the bus pull in Grade 10. But most of the homages came in The Six-Month Backslide.

It took me a long time to write *The Six-Month Backslide*. The reason is because I lost two very close friends of mine just over a month apart and it took me a while to get to the place where I could try to be funny again.

My friend David Widdicombe was a beautiful man and a writing colleague. He always gave me the best notes and advice on my work. I was looking for a backdrop to set the 6th story against and I had a flash of inspiration one night. I could set it at a funeral and base it on his good friend Ross whom David looked after. Ross was in his 90's and we used to take him out for dinner regularly. This ice cream story in Backslide was Ross through and through. So I thought to myself, I'll have to give David a shout and see if he thinks it's okay if I act on this latest flash of inspiration. The next day I received news that he had passed away. I am certain, that inspiration came from David who tapped me on the shoulder and said, "Go get 'em big boy."

The following month, I lost one of my best friends from high school through today in Dr. Stephen Moore. He wasn't a chemist but rather had a Ph.D. in medieval literature. Steve was the kindest, funniest, smartest guy I've ever known. A really wonderful person. So I wanted to pay tribute to his memory by naming the teacher character after him. The teacher was loosely based on W R D Coffey who passed away earlier this year. He was my history teacher all through high school.

So I hope you will indulge me sharing these memories of my friends and how they influenced the last story in the book.

As for the future, I plan to write another volume of The New Twenty stories as I not so subtly hinted at the very end of this one. But please don't ask me when. I want to start working on a straight out new novel which I plan to start in early 2018. And then probably Volume II will come after that.

To the loyal readers and fans, again I sincerely thank you for all of your love and support.

Made in the USA
Middletown, DE
27 April 2018